SPECIAL MESSAGE TO READERS

This book is published under the auspices of

THE ULVERSCROFT FOUNDATION

(registered charity No. 264873 UK)

Established in 1972 to provide funds for research, diagnosis and treatment of eye diseases. Examples of contributions made are: —

A Children's Assessment Unit at Moorfield's Hospital, London.

•

Twin operating theatres at the Western Ophthalmic Hospital, London.

•

A Chair of Ophthalmology at the Royal Australian College of Ophthalmologists.

•

The Ulverscroft Children's Eye Unit at the Great Ormond Street Hospital For Sick Children, London.

You can help further the work of the Foundation by making a donation or leaving a legacy. Every contribution, no matter how small, is received with gratitude. Please write for details to:

THE ULVERSCROFT FOUNDATION,
The Green, Bradgate Road, Anstey,
Leicester LE7 7FU, England.
Telephone: (0116) 236 4325

In Australia write to:
THE ULVERSCROFT FOUNDATION,
c/o The Royal Australian and New Zealand College of Ophthalmologists,
94-98 Chalmers Street, Surry Hills,
N.S.W. 2010, Australia

THE CAPTAIN'S CREEK

Maggie's solitary life is interrupted when she discovers an exhausted stranger on the beach, hiding from the press gang pursuing him. With her father away at sea, she trusts her own intuition, and risks sheltering the man. Little does Maggie realise that this rash act will jeopardise her plans to open up a school with her trusted friend, Hester. For the handsome stranger, Montgomery, is a man led by his own private mission . . .

Books by Valerie Holmes in the Linford Romance Library:

THE MASTER OF MONKTON MANOR
THE KINDLY LIGHT
HANNAH OF HARPHAM HALL
PHOEBE'S CHALLENGE
BETRAYAL OF INNOCENCE
AMELIA'S KNIGHT
OBERON'S CHILD
REBECCA'S REVENGE

VALERIE HOLMES

THE CAPTAIN'S CREEK

Complete and Unabridged

LINFORD
Leicester

First published in Great Britain in 2007

First Linford Edition
published 2007

British Library CIP Data

Holmes, Valerie
The captain's creek.—Large print ed.—
Linford romance library
1. Love stories
2. Large type books
I. Title
823.9′2 [F]

ISBN 978–1–84617–907–5

Published by
F. A. Thorpe (Publishing)
Anstey, Leicestershire

Set by Words & Graphics Ltd.
Anstey, Leicestershire
Printed and bound in Great Britain by
T. J. International Ltd., Padstow, Cornwall

This book is printed on acid-free paper

1

Maggie took off her boots, hitched up her skirts and tiptoed into the icy cold water as it trickled over stones and boulders making its way out into the North Sea.

This was a quiet spot, lonely even, but Maggie loved it because it was unspoilt, almost unknown to all but the oldest families of the village, and to her.

She cherished every moment there because it represented freedom. The woodland slopes at either side of the steep gill made this little creek appear as if from nowhere, like a mystical place. It opened out onto the beach behind the headland, sheltered from the worst of the assaults by the wind and tide.

Spring was warming up and moving nearer the summer months and, with longer, brighter days, Maggie's spirit lifted with renewed hope that she would be trusted or respected by the townsfolk at last.

The depth of her own winter despair behind her, there was only her own future to consider, which included the children of the village, Telby, if only the people would trust her. Soon she would start her own school.

The villagers would learn to accept her and all would be well. Hadn't she helped them all through the damage of the storms and after three men were lost on the wrecked ship last month? Even Hester Ramsdale, an important local figure, short, austere and hard as nails, had made her a pot of tea after that and brought her a cake in a gesture of thanks.

Maggie's mother, bless her soul, had not lived to see the day their school house would open but she, Margaret Louise Chase, was determined to see her mother's plan fulfilled.

She breathed deeply letting the fresh sea air refresh her body and soul. The stream flowed steady and strong. Its current was quite slow today unlike when the rains came, and this seemingly harmless babbling brook could turn into a raging torrent.

But it had not rained in days so she took a series of little delicate hops from stone to stone to cross the narrow creek to the other side, where she could walk around the low cliff and onto the flat expanse of sandy beach. It was in this state of pleasant euphoria that she skipped across the mouth of the creek . . . and slipped.

As her body plunged into a pool of water some three feet deep, slowed on its way down to the sea by two large rocks, she gasped as the cold enveloped her. It took only a second for her feet to find the shingle on its sandy bed, but it seemed much longer to her as she struggled to lift herself from the water's grip.

Maggie's feet felt the ground and she was instantly able to propel her head up out of the water, gasping for air and shivering as her hands groped the rocks to hold firmly against the flow of the water's pull. With all pretence at grace forgotten, she threw her soaking boots over to the sandy shore, heaved herself and her heavy skirts free and crawled hand and foot from one rock to the other as she clambered onto the small beach below the cliff.

Once standing there, sodden and shaken, she looked around her for any sign that someone else may have witnessed her foolery and, when all seemed natural and quiet, she laughed out loud at her own clumsiness, but rapidly made her way to where the sun's warmth had dried out the fine sand.

Maggie raised her face to the warmth of its rays, standing silently for a moment knowing she now had a big problem. She would not dry out as quickly as the loose grains beneath her feet and she had to return to her cottage to change her clothes.

Why, Maggie wondered, was no idea

she ever had as straight forward as it appeared to be once she carried it through?

She sat down, spreading her skirts as wide as she could and looked over the waves to a distant horizon. Maggie thought that she may as well see if some of the material would dry out, but she would have to curtail her walk and return to her cottage before the sun lost its power. Restless and frustrated, she was determined to at least walk a little way onto the beach, as she had come so far.

She dragged herself upright, cursing the sand that now stuck to the back of her skirts making them heavy and cumbersome, and walked around the small headland climbing over the boulders that hid the creek from the main bay, and froze as her eyes fell upon two separate things.

A body had fallen between the boulders, with blood upon his arm. He looked as though he, too, had slipped and fallen, hitting his head upon the rock — the body still breathed. His wrist was marked with a red ring, a tell-tale sign that this man had been cuffed or bound. In the distance, soldiers were running along the bay toward the headland. Maggie glanced towards the sea.

The tide was for turning and coming back in. It would hinder the soldiers' progress but not quickly enough to stop them from reaching this injured man.

She tugged at the man's jacket. He did not look like a ruffian. In fact his clothes were quite fine. 'Are you dead, man?'

Maggie realised this was a stupid thing to ask as he would hardly reply if he were. The tide lapped in between the huge immovable rocks and washed over the man's boots. He groaned as he stirred and looked up at her, fear in his eyes. 'I might be, miss, or are you an angel?' His voice was deep and sounded educated, no trace of a local accent.

'There are soldiers approaching. Do you know them?' Maggie asked, and once again realised her words were coming out all wrong.

'Not personally.' He sat up, grimaced and held his arm. She stopped him from peering over the boulder. 'Is there anywhere to hide around here?' he asked, his eyes searched her face as if pleading for her to say, 'yes'.

Maggie looked around her. There was no time to head up to the creek. If the men were not local and had knowledge of it, then she knew it would be better she did not lead them to it. The cliff was too steep for him to climb and the sea would be far too exposed to musket fire.

'Can you curl up tightly into a ball between these rocks, and stay there perfectly still?' she asked, not knowing why she should conspire to help the man. He could be a murderer for all she knew, or a complete wastrel. But something about him told her he was neither and she, after all, was a creature that followed her instincts.

'Yes, I can, but they will still see me.'

He put a hand on hers as it rested on the rock. 'They will kill me if they take me. Please help me. They are a press gang — I'm no criminal.'

'No, they will not. But stay perfectly still, one is quite near. Say no more.'

He painfully cradled his legs. Maggie saw the grimace cross his face and she felt so sorry for his predicament. Once he had tucked his feet as neatly in as he could she sat upon one rock and spread her heavy skirts across the other, letting one leg and her skirt fall over the stranger's head and knees. He was completely hidden, but she felt him shivering as the tide trickled in and out between the rocks and his body.

The soldier climbed over the boulders strewn along the bay and looked at her in amazement, as if he had stumbled upon a mermaid fresh out of the sea.

'You gave me quite a start, sir!' she snapped back, hugging her boots to her.

'I could say the same . . . miss.' He looked at her searchingly. 'You're all wet.'

'Yes, sir. I am all wet, but hopefully the sun will dry my clothes before I return to my home. I fell in you see.' She pointed to the sea and looked down with embarrassment, but really she was checking that her skirts had not slipped revealing the man's boots hidden underneath.

'Have you seen a man run past these rocks?' He looked at her, barely hiding his amusement at her bedraggled appearance.

'No-one, sir. Or I should not be sitting here in this state.' She looked defiantly back up at him, then asked, 'Who is it that you seek? And why?'

'We seek a ruffian, miss, who is a coward and a disgrace to his country. He has refused to do his duty and serve in His Majesty's Navy. But if I get my hands on him I'll have the skin off his back first for the trouble he has caused us.' The man looked around him, and then saw the look of horror on Maggie's face as she listened to his words.

'Beggin' yer pardon, miss, but these

are hard times. He not only shot through our guard, but he let out eight other men, too. A whole night's work gone to waste and now word will be out that we're here.' The man was staring back along the cliffs.

2

'You are a press gang?' Maggie asked innocently, trying not to show the disgust she felt for them. They were loathed locally because they stole away the village's men and boys whenever they swept along this stretch of the north-east coast in their raids.

Mostly, the men they took were from fishing families and as such were needed to provide food for their families, but the gangs were greedy and did not listen to the people's pleas. In some villages the gangs themselves were attacked and so raids hereabouts were now rare.

'Aye, lass, we are, and I suggest if you see this man you had better run the other way. He's both violent and dangerous, and I daresay I'd toss a coin in your direction of you send word to the Cock's Crow Inn on the moor road should you see a stranger in these parts.' The soldier smiled at her as she flicked a wet curl from her face. 'You'd best be getting home before you catch a chill.'

Maggie forced herself to smile back at him as if she was impressed by his offer. 'Thank you for your concern, but I shall stay here and enjoy the sunshine for a few minutes more whilst you find your man.'

'Is there any way he could have got up there, along the cliff from this stretch of beach?' The soldier was obviously puzzled as he had seen the stranger run part way along the beach.

'Oh yes, easily. If you go back about fifty yards, there are the old steps carved into the cliff. They were at one time used for the fishing boats, but not in recent years. They are a bit risky, but someone who was young, fit and desperate could climb up them still.' Maggie watched the colour of the man's face turn puce.

'Damnation! Whilst we're blithering

here, he's up there and headed for the open road. Good day, miss.' He ran back down the beach, shouting orders to the four men who were following on behind him.

Maggie waited until they were out of sight then moved quickly aside.

Dark troubled eyes stared back at her from a very pale face.

'Can you move?' she asked him, concern rising as to what she'd do if he couldn't.

Slowly he stretched out a long leg, then the other. 'Yes,' was the weary reply.

'Then stay low. I shall stand here whilst you roll or crawl over the rock. Once on the soft sand at the other side, stay down. We shall make for the creek, but we shall have to help each other to cross it safely; those stones are treacherously slippery.'

He sat up and touched her skirts. 'You speak from experience, I see?'

'Yes, can I suggest you hurry? If they return, I think they would not stop at removing the skin from your back. You seem to have really upset them.'

Maggie watched as he almost rolled himself over the rock and made his way to the cliff base, gripping his wounded arm.

She walked over to him and, as soon as they were sheltered by the headland, she placed an arm around the man's back, lifting his good arm across her own shoulders, enabling them to move more swiftly down to the creek.

Maggie's boots were balanced in one of her hands. He took them from her and, with strength and accuracy, threw them with all his might to the other side of the stretch of water.

They both made their way across the creek. No hopping this time. They were soaked to the skin, so together they plodded through the water, steadying each other as they went, only stopping when Maggie retrieved her boots and she and the stranger were safely hidden in the woodland at the other side.

Maggie shivered as, out of the sun's

warmth, the shady path was cold. Her sodden garments were heavy and icy to the touch. The man put his good arm around her waist gripping her firmly and pulling her in to his side. She pulled away sharply, turning to face him.

'What do you think you are doing?' she asked, shivering and indignant.

'Trying to keep us both warm whilst we walk to wherever it is we are going,' he replied in a lowered voice while his body shivered involuntarily.

Maggie could see he had acted in earnest. 'I'm sorry,' she explained, 'But I am not used to being manhandled.' Maggie felt her choice of words was definitely lacking judgement this day.

He smiled back at her. 'I am relieved to hear that, but this is not a normal event for either of us, so can I ask that we hurry together, as best that we are able, to a place of safety? You do know of one, don't you?'

Maggie did indeed know of one. Her own home, but she was not sure she wanted to share it with this stranger. She hesitated, just for a moment of indecision, and he leaned against a tree. His eyes were half closed and he breathed deeply. She saw the trickle of blood run down his hand from his wound.

'Yes, yes, I do and you are quite right, we must hurry.' She linked arms with the man and made straight for her own home, her place of peace away from the troubles of the world but, as she glanced at the strong features of the stranger, something told her those days were gone.

3

The cottage that was now Maggie's own home had been standing at the top of the steep wooded bank that rose from the creek for over a hundred years. It was known by the villagers, but never considered by them to be a part of Telby.

Exhausted from the climb, she sat the stranger down on the old makeshift bench that her father had made for her and her mother before he had left them. From here, the two women could look out over the sea in all its moods, wondering at its beauty, waiting for him to return to them. Maggie had no time now for such reflection.

She sat next to the man whilst they caught their breath. The ascent was steep, but with the weight of an injured man pulling against her, what was usually an exhilarating walk had turned into an ordeal.

'The cottage is just there.' Maggie pointed behind her, realising that the seclusion and peace that it normally offered, was now a risk in itself. She knew nothing of this man other than that he had escaped a press gang and had allowed others to, also.

To her it appeared a noble act, although her father may have strongly disagreed with her, but he was not here to advise her, so she had to use her own judgement.

The man turned his head a little stiffly, looking back over his shoulder. Along a narrow path, which led from the vantage point through to the end of the woods, was her cottage. Built long and quite low, it was well established, undisturbed by time. Unlike the red pantiled roofs of the bay towns, this one had a dull grey weather-worn roof that blended in well with the surrounding countryside as, behind it, woodland gave way to the moorland.

'This is your family home?' the stranger spoke. He was looking quite pale and his speech had lost some of its eloquence as he gasped the words out.

'Yes, come on now. We must get you in there before we both freeze in our sodden clothes.' Maggie hooked her arm under his and helped him to his feet. His stance was shaky, but he gritted his teeth and pushed onwards.

4

Maggie was glad that her fire would still be burning in the hearth, keeping the cottage warm. Together they stumbled the last few yards, arm in arm, and almost fell on to the threshold as she unlatched the old wooden door.

Inside, all was neat and homely. A stew pot hung over the slow burning fire filling the room with a pleasant aroma. A half-made clip mat was left strewn across a wooden rocking chair by the fire.

A finely embroidered lace tablecloth covered a square oak table by the window. Maggie swiftly moved the rug clippings and let the stranger flop down into the chair. The warmth of the fire desperately needed to breathe life back into his pale face.

'Thank you, miss.' His voice was low, his eyes closed as he sat motionless in the chair. 'You must excuse my ill manners. I have not slept nor eaten for nearly two days.'

'You have no reason to apologise to me, sir, for being so victimised. Besides, you should not waste your breath thanking me for my help. What else could I do?' Maggie answered, dismissing his gratitude as she scooped out two bowls worth of broth from the pot, placing them on the flagstone by the fire.

Maggie walked over to a chest that was wedged against a whitewashed wall. She opened it and pulled out a pair of her father's trousers, a shirt and long jacket. Hugging them to her for a moment, she felt the sense of guilt fade from her as she looked at the slumped figure by her fire. Her father would understand surely, if he knew. Maggie told herself that she was certain he would, dismissing her doubtful thoughts.

She placed the garments down carefully on top of the clip mat by the stranger's feet. 'What is your name?' she asked, as she gently tapped his unhurt arm, to bring his attention back to a conscious level.

He picked up one of the bowls and gratefully sipped the warm broth. He seemed to savour it with relish and eagerly took another mouthful before answering her.

'Montgomery,' he answered, without taking his eyes off the broth until it had all gone. His eyelids immediately looked heavy. The fire seemed to be lulling him back to sleep.

'Well, Montgomery, you are going to have to help me in order that I may help you further. I'm going to change quickly and you have to also.' He forced his eyes open, looking at the clothes by his feet. 'Are they your husband's?' he asked.

'No, my father's,' she answered, and ran down a narrow corridor from the parlour to what had been her parents' room, but was now her own. Quick as she could she unfastened her dress and let it drop to the floor. It was a relief to have the cold weight fall from her tired body.

Wrapping a blanket around herself she fetched out another dress. It was finer than she would normally wear around the cottage but her working dress was in a mangled heap on the floor. She pulled out one of her mother's warm shawls and a pair of her embroidered slippers. It only took her a moment to dress.

In a cupboard she found some off-cuts of linen and tore them into strips, they would do to bandage his wound. She picked up a bowl from the scullery and poured hot water into it from the kettle by the fire. A jar of salve made with honey was collected from the cold store as she ran back to her injured guest, Montgomery. A grand name, she decided, for someone who appeared to be an outlaw.

He had removed his jacket and opened his shirt, but had not managed to slip it over his muscular chest and arms. 'I . . . ' he looked down slightly, 'I shall be fine like this thank you. The fire will warm me through in no time.'

'Let me help you.' Maggie pulled the shirt carefully over his head then peeled it off gently over his wounded arm. She looked at the angry gash. The bullet had winged him, but it had not been a direct enough hit to in-bed itself deeply into his flesh or bone. He had been very fortunate indeed.

She wasted no time in cleaning and binding the wound with the salve. He grimaced, but did not moan or complain. However, Maggie was shocked when she saw his back.

The remains of a beating he had recently endured were clear to see. No doubt, she thought, at the press gang's hands. His back was a mass of bruises. 'I'll rub some liniment into these, it may help.' This she did, and aided him to dress in her father's shirt and coat. She pulled off his boots then looked at him.

His face was flushed, either by the warmth from the flames or by her intimacy, or perhaps shame that his fine figure had been abused so by the ruffians in uniform. 'I think you should do the next bit yourself, whilst I cut you some ham and make us some tea.'

He nodded his agreement as she handed him the breeches and a length of rope, her father's girth was more ample than that of her new friend. She pointedly turned her back to him as he struggled in and out of the breeches.

'Here, try this.' He drank keenly of the tea, but ate very little. She moved the frame of a cot bed from the narrow cupboard in the passage to the floor near the fire. She reached into the cupboard behind the open stairs and retrieved a mattress.

This was then unrolled and placed on top of the bed, filled with the remnants of wool from the local sheep; it was plumped up and softened. Her mother hated the horse-hair or straw-filled ones that were commonly used.

'Rest here,' she said. Without hesitation he gratefully flopped down on to it, his energy spent.

Maggie brought him a quilted blanket and wrapped it around his body. He placed a hand upon hers as she tucked the material carefully around his chest. 'I will repay your kindness, miss. You have no idea of the importance of your actions today. For what you have done has not only spared me my life — you have saved it, and the cause, and others.' He released her hand.

'I did what anyone of decent character would have done in the same circumstance, I am quite sure,' Maggie said, and gently tucked his hand back under the covers.

'No, miss, you did more than that, you risked your own freedom.' He closed his eyes and looked as peaceful as a child in slumber. She stroked his brow automatically, then stood up rather quickly as the familiarity and ease with which she had welcomed this stranger into her home surprised her.

'What cause?' she asked, a little unnerved at the gravity of his words.

But if he heard her question, he gave no reply. Maggie dropped the latch on the cottage door and closed the shutters. She left their boots to dry out at a distance from the direct heat of the fire.

Maggie retired to her parents' bed, cold, tired and with a heavy head. She had more questions than answers regarding the man who lay in her own bed, but for now they both needed warmth and sleep. Tomorrow she would ask him again.

5

Maggie slept longer than she had intended to. When she awoke it was already the early hours of the morning and at first she thought she had been dreaming.

The memories of the man, Montgomery, appeared to her as a blurred impossibility until she saw her own wet dress hanging in the corner, then all was remembered vividly.

She rose with excitement and anticipation. Who was her guest? What was his cause? She could not wait to find out. Wrapped in a shawl around her shoulders she slipped her feet into her mother's silk slippers. They had been a gift from her father after he had been on one of his long trips.

Throughout her life he had been no more than a vague figure, going away for months at a time, then arriving back unannounced expecting her to hug and respond to him as a daughter should, but he was, to her, almost a stranger. When he did arrive home he would always have gifts for them and tales of strange lands and people of different colour and faiths. Heathens, he called them, but they fascinated her none-the-less.

Now his ship was being used as a transport to the colonies, to the new lands across the mighty oceans. He had been gone nearly sixteen months already, in which time Mother had died. Now, she had to wait for his return, a man who was more like an acquaintance to her than a relative. That worried her; it played with her mind, in her dreams as much as the loneliness she felt after her mother's passing, but for now she had more immediate concerns.

Tip-toeing over the cold flagstones she peeped around the door into the parlour. The cot bed was there, where she remembered placing it, but it was made up neatly, and empty.

Maggie felt strangely disappointed. Her unexpected visitor was a mystery she had wanted to solve. Who and what was he? What was his cause? Her mind was filled with the same two questions that it appeared would not be answered.

She opened the cottage door and looked out towards the woods. Shadows were dark, created by the bright moonlight. The cold breeze that blew in made her gasp, as it came straight off an icy northern sea.

'I wouldn't stand there too long, miss, you'll catch your death.' The voice, deep and gentle, surprised her.

She spun around to see Montgomery standing in the parlour doorway. He had to stoop slightly under the low beam. The initial inhabitants of the cottage must have been far smaller than men of today, she thought.

He held up a tankard to her. 'I hope you don't mind, but I awoke and was devilishly thirsty. I helped myself to some ale, but I will repay it threefold as soon as I am able to.'

Maggie closed and bolted the door. 'You are welcome to it, sir,' she answered. It seemed presumptuous to call a stranger by his Christian name yet this whole situation was most unusual and would destroy her reputation should the townsfolk find out. Then there would be no school, not to be run by a fallen woman, as she would be called by the old gossips.

He entered the parlour and, as if reading her thoughts, replied, 'Please, don't worry yourself, I shall leave. I shall not inconvenience you any more than I need to. May I get you a drink?' For the first time he grinned and his serious persona was lost to a boyish charm.

'I can get my own drink, but thank you for asking.' Maggie walked over to the table but hesitated for a moment before sitting down.

'Please do not fear me. I will not harm you in any way. I have only thanks and gratitude for the risk you took to protect me down there on the beach.' He sat down at the table with her.

'I do not fear you,' she said, and stared defiantly back into his deep blue eyes.

'Perhaps not, which is just as well for me, but a worry, for you are in a very vulnerable position up here on your own.'

Maggie wanted to reply defensively as many of the locals had thought the same, but it was her home and, without it, she would be at the mercy of some household's good nature — something that she thought was in short supply as the villagers were a close knit community. They had their secrets and didn't let strangers become too close.

Her mother had thought the fishing village would be a fine place to be based as it had no school and was just being joined by a new road, the York — Newcastle coastal road, thereby guaranteeing future growth as accessibility grew. What had been seen as a huge opportunity to her mother had been seen as a threat by the local people, who regarded even the townspeople beyond the headland as total strangers.

The newly-built vicarage had been offered as a place where she could stay and work to help the Reverend's wife, a thought that had made her want to retreat to her own home even more. But her father must return to her soon, for she could not sell the cottage or rent it out without his consent, so she stayed put.

'What cause did you speak of last night?' she asked, and saw his hand hesitate as he lifted the tankard up towards his lips.

'Cause?' he raised a quizzical eyebrow.

'Yes, you said I saved you and the cause . . . What cause?' she persisted.

He placed the tankard down on the table and yawned.

'Sorry, I must still be tired. I think you misheard me, or I perhaps mumbled something as I fell to sleep. I think I must have said, 'You saved my life, of course.'

He walked back over to the bed. 'I was almost delirious after all. If you would indulge me further, I should like to sleep some more.'

Maggie knew he had not said anything of the sort, but whatever his secret was it was equally obvious that he did not intend to share it with her — yet. 'Of course, sir. You must sleep. I shall not disturb you for a few more hours.' She left him and went to her room and dressed in readiness for the morning, waiting to quiz her guest once more.

Once the sun was high in the sky and its rays lit another day, Maggie decided it was now time to disturb Montgomery once more. She chose a dress that, although made of a strong cotton weave, was a pastel blue that would show off the similar colour of her eyes and her dark blonde hair.

She excused herself such a frivolous action because her work dress was still so wet. She could see light from the parlour as she walked down the passage.

6

'Good morning, Mont . . . ' she stepped inside the room, stopping in her tracks as she saw the rolled up mattress, and her father's clothes, except his shirt, neatly folded on the bed. There was no trace that he had ever been. She walked over to the chair by the fire and gently rocked it to and fro with one finger, staring at it as if she was in a trance.

Maggie had kept herself very busy since her mother had died, to keep the loneliness at bay, but it seemed to suddenly engulf her. For a few hours she had felt useful, needed even, and it was a feeling she had relished.

She ate some bread with the broth. It warmed her and chased away her dismal feelings. 'Hester' she said to herself, 'I think it is time I returned your favour.' She set to, baking some scones. Once done, she tidied her hair and put on her mother's boots. Fortunately they had been of similar size.

Maggie was just about to leave the cottage when something shiny caught her eye. A shiny button had been left in the centre of the table. It was silver and had engraved upon it an anchor and chain.

She turned it over in her hand and saw that it had been engraved on the reverse, *M.F.M.* Was it a clue? *Montgomery. F.M*? Or was it left as some means of payment? She had no idea, but one thing was certain, she was going to keep it safe until she had all her answers.

Placing it carefully in the deep pocket in her skirt, she then put the scones in the cloth, and then into her basket. Another thought crossed her mind — perhaps he was telling her that he would return. Maggie hoped so, she would like to know that he was all right.

She walked at a pace along the track that led to the Telby road. Normally, she would take the shortcut and walk along the beach, but she had a good dress on and didn't want to risk getting her only other decent pair of boots wet. Maggie had not been on the road very long before she saw the Reverend Higgs driving his gig down the road. He waved to her and pulled up alongside.

'Miss Chase, can I give you a lift to town?' he greeted her warmly. He was such a stark contrast to his wife. Where she was timid and watchful, the Reverend Higgs was warm in his manner, friendly by nature. He had won the villagers over in a comparatively short time.

'Yes, thank you. I'm calling on Mrs Ramsdale. I've baked her some scones,' she said, and passed them up to him whilst she climbed up alongside him on the seat. He sniffed the air above the basket and said, 'They smell beautiful, quite makes me hungry, Maggie. May I call you Maggie?'

'Yes, of course. Would you like one? I've made plenty.' She peeled back the cloth and watched with pride as he placed the reins in his other hand and gratefully took one.

'Oh, delicious!' He ate the scone with appreciation and paid her the highest compliment he could have, without knowing it. 'They're as good as your late mother's, bless her soul.' As the gig moved forward slowly, he seemed in no hurry to return to Telby. He let the horse walk on at its own casual pace.

'Tell me, Maggie, how is life in the cottage? Are you coping on your own?' He looked at her, and she was touched by his genuine concern.

'Yes, I really am, but I would dearly love to help the children in the town.' She watched him as he chuckled.

'Hence, the scones for the outspoken Mrs Ramsdale. You are a wise young woman and so like your dear determined mother. However, you are both making a very big mistake.'

'What is that?' Maggie asked. She looked up at the profile of the man, noticing the Romanesque outline of his nose, on which was propped the small circular glasses, giving him a learned look. Even his now greying hair had a similar effect as it curled naturally around his face. The longer hair was pulled back and tied by a string of leather at the nape of his neck.

'Have you given any thought as to why she and some of the other townsfolk are so scared of you educating their youngsters?' He stopped the gig and looked most earnestly at her.

'Yes, because I am a stranger and they don't like outsiders, do they?' Her question was, she hoped, an opportunity for him to open up to her, for they had at least that in common.

'They are scared of the unknown, the new, it represents a challenge. They have been a community for hundreds of years. These local villagers have not travelled far, except the menfolk, and that is across the sea. But it is not you that is the threat to them, Maggie. It is literally the unknown. What will you be teaching their young children?' He raised a quizzical brow.

'Why, to read and write, of course . . . and the scriptures.' She blushed slightly not wanting to sound as if she were doing more than she should and infringing on his own duties.

'Indeed, the scriptures they may be familiar with, if they have listened to me at all, but who has taught them to read and write?'

Maggie was taken aback. The obvious reason for their resentment had never occurred to her. Many were themselves illiterate. The new people who came to trade with them and who were considering setting up new establishments to expand the town were all more educated than the local people. That was the real threat to them. They, in their eyes, would always be the underdogs, except at sea.

'Then I shall teach the adults first!' Maggie said, filled with renewed enthusiasm. She saw clearly that she had a mission of her own to fulfil. If they would forget their pride and place their trust in her she could help them to provide services that would be needed in a developing town.

'I think you had better handle Hester with great care, Maggie,' The Reverend advised and looked at her above his spectacles. 'Win her over and you are half way there. Unfortunately, my good lady wife adopted a different approach and has not had a great deal of success in this matter, but you are different. It may be the Lord will use you where others have tried and failed, but you possess something that they lacked.

'Determination?' Maggie offered as a possible adjective he may use, remembering she had been called stubborn many times over by her mother.

'No, that was not what I had in mind, as my wife was very determined to bring Hester in line. No, it was passion, Maggie. You are full of it and driven with it.' He smiled at her as she was taken aback by his words. 'Maggie, passion can be a destroyer of beauty or a builder of grace. Use it wisely and it will take you far.'

He looked back to the road ahead and flicked the reins. They moved forward a pace, in quiet reflection as she thought deeply over his words and the challenge that she needed to meet. What a challenge, she thought excitedly as he pulled up outside Hester's cottage.

'Thank you, Reverend,' she said as he passed down her basket.

'Remember, passion tempered, but not stopped by wisdom.'

'Thank you, I shall meet the challenge.' She smiled back at him.

'I'm sure you will. God Bless you, Maggie.'

She watched him drive on and felt a surge of comfort as she had at least one friend who understood her. Then she saw the curtain in the cottage waver and knew she had been seen. Hester had seen her and hopefully she would listen to her words.

7

Montgomery crouched down low behind the old stone wall. He'd been running in the darkness for nearly three hours before morning broke. His body had been telling him it was loathe to leave the warmth of the cottage as his muscles and wound ached at the beating they had had.

Then there was the pretty owner, a young woman apparently left on her own in such an inhospitable place. She had a smile that had warmed his heart as her heart had warmed his body, battered as it was. But his brain had forced him to face the harsh reality of his situation and, reluctantly he had dressed in his still damp clothes, except for his shirt, that he could not manage.

How he cursed his ill luck, he had nearly missed the shot, but it had caught his arm. Walking, running or stumbling as far as he could he had followed the shadows of hedges, walls or woods and finally managed to reach his friend, Theodore's, little piece of heaven on earth. He followed the perimeter of the graveyard until he was no more than ten yards from the vestry door at the back of the old Norman church.

Montgomery ran almost on all fours to it, with a feeling of relief flooding over him as he turned the large iron ring that had served for centuries as the handle on the old oak door. The surprised face of the curate who was just removing his robes greeted him as he entered slamming the door firmly shut behind him.

'Montgomery! I thought they had taken you away.' Theodore moved forward to give his friend a hug of welcome as the man was obviously greatly relieved to see him. Montgomery stepped back before his enthusiastic friend crushed his sore arm in his friendly grip. 'Are you injured?' the curate asked.

Montgomery leaned on the door and put the heavy latch in position.

'They did catch me, Theodore, and eight other men. Damn them! Everything I've worked towards for the last ten months was ruined in one stupid moment of brutality. We were lucky, though. I managed to jump one guard as he sat drinking brandy, fresh off a boat I'll be bound. We dispersed to the four winds as soon as we were free.

'There was no time to arrange anything and the meeting had not even begun in earnest before the press gang arrived and it fell apart, and now we're scattered all over North Yorkshire. It will take some time to regroup. Confidence has been smashed, Theo, instead of the machines they intended to break in the mills. All I can do is stay around the area and slowly try to build up the contacts again. No-one knew if that press gang was a coincidence or *too much* of a coincidence.'

He slumped down onto a hard

wooden chair. ‘As the new man, I will be the major suspect of treachery, if they, as I do, think that it could have been arranged. I hope they don’t gang together and decide I am a traitor to their cause or I will be hiding from both the authorities and the men. If they find out who I am I will definitely be murdered unless I take a boat to the colonies!’

‘Now calm yourself, Monty. You surely are taking this too far. No-one knows of your involvement except me and Douglas. I am certain he would never say a word out of turn. It is beyond belief.

‘Even if it takes another six months you must persevere and arrange another meeting. They have to be stopped before it is too late. Your father cannot last forever but equally, whilst he still draws breath, he will not change his ways. You have fallen foul of his temper with your revolutionary ideas, now you must earn the respect of the men and protect them at the same time. We have to make them see sense or else the whole country will turn to anarchy! We will have an English Revolution and blood in our streets, too.' Theodore slammed his fist onto the table to stress his point. Montgomery laughed.

'Theo, your sermons never lack either passion or fire. We're not French, the revolution will not happen here.' Montgomery could see the disbelief on Theodore's face.

'Don't be too sure, Montgomery. People have changed. The farming communities have been decimated by this new shift to mills and factories. People don't care about each other like they used to, the world is driven by money and the rich become richer as the people are becoming poorer.' Theodore poured his friend a glass of red wine.

'Isn't that for the Holy Communion?' Montgomery asked.

'Then consider yourself blessed, Montgomery. Now let me tend to your arm.' Theodore moved the sleeve of the shirt carefully until he could see the neatly-fastened bandage wrapped carefully around the wound. 'You are either extremely resourceful or you have made a new friend.' He raised his eyebrows at Montgomery as he rolled back the shirt fabric to his friend's wrist.

'I was helped by someone who still does care about the underdog,' Montgomery said, but did not offer any further explanation. For some reason the vulnerability of Maggie was paramount in his mind. The fewer people who knew of her involvement the safer it would be for her. Besides which, if he needed somewhere to hide, that no one else knew about, not even Theodore, Maggie's cottage provided him with the perfect place.

'By whom?' Theodore asked, as he put on his black coat and hat.

'I don't rightly know . . . ' Montgomery stood up, avoiding looking at his friend directly. 'It was a helpful stranger. I wasn't in a position to ask many questions.'

‘Male or female?’ Theodore persevered sounding more than a little unconvinced.

‘Theo, the less you know the less you will have to lie if you are questioned by anyone and therefore the clearer your conscience will be.’ Montgomery was pleased he had come up with a plausible reason not to divulge Maggie’s identity.

‘Intriguing,’ Theodore answered. ‘However, we have to decide how we get you safely out of here and over to the vicarage before anyone else sees you, my friend.’

‘A disguise,’ Montgomery suggested.

‘Excellent idea!’ Theodore exclaimed, and stared around the vestry at the tall cupboard in which his and Douglas’s robes were hung. ‘Here, you take my hat, coat, and my stick and I’ll wear a cassock. Then if we are seen together they may even think I am walking with Douglas.’

‘Good,’ Montgomery said and smiled as he placed the unfamiliar hat upon his head. The men exchanged clothes and set off down the old rickety path to the vicarage beyond the graveyard. Montgomery held a small Bible in his hand and looked down at the overgrown path as they walked along, as if deep in conversation with each other. They arrived at the vicarage as Douglas pulled up in his gig by the gates.

'Good morning, Theodore, I was not expecting guests this morning. Who is it we have the pleasure of . . . ' Douglas's words ceased as Montgomery looked up, showing his face from under the hat's broad brim. 'Heaven's above, you are safe! Come inside, you must get yourself out of sight before you are seen and word travels around the village. I shall tell my wife we have a guest. Theodore, take Montgomery into the parlour. I shall join you there.' Douglas disappeared into the house.

Theodore led Montgomery inside. The dark corridor led to a cluster of doors; two to the right, two to the left and a staircase and door straight ahead. Although the walls were painted in a fashionable pastel green, there was so little light allowed in that the area was gloomy and dark. The small parlour to the right was sparse of furnishings unlike Maggie's homely cottage.

The chairs in here were hard, with straight solid backs. All the neatly-worked samplers on the wall displayed the *Word of the Lord*. A fire burned low in the grate so as to take the initial chill off the room, but it was not built up high to emit sufficient heat as to warm the room completely through like the glowing hearth of Maggie's cottage.

Nothing that was overtly comforting except for the embroidered *Word* was on show in this family room. It was basic, functional and severe, like the lady of the house who had created it.

When Douglas returned to them, his wife who was dressed in a dowdy dark brown dress followed behind him. She stared at Montgomery for a moment down her long chiselled nose and he stood immediately offering her the seat he had occupied nearest the fire's limited warmth.

'Thank you . . . sir,' she answered, as she sat down in her usual seat, but there was no smile, nor humour in her response.

'Montgomery, we have a room at the back of the house that you are welcome to stay in whilst you decide what your next journey will be,' Douglas offered and Montgomery could not help but notice that his friend was avoiding eye contact with his wife.

Theodore stood awkwardly against the wall of the room trying to appear at ease as he stared out of the window; his presence had been acknowledged by the woman's curt nod, but then she had frowned at the mud on both his and Montgomery's boots.

'That is very kind of you, but I fear I must be moving on. Perhaps I could trouble you for a meal and . . . ' Montgomery hesitated and looked down suddenly feeling awkward. He did not like to ask for some coin as an advance until he could obtain some of his own money however much he needed his friends to lend him some.

The press gang had relieved him of his purse. The presence of Douglas's wife, Leticia, made everything feel rather difficult. It did not seem fitting for him to mention such matters within her hearing.

'Are you damp, sir?' her sharp voice asked accusingly as she watched some moist air rise from his trouser leg as he was standing next to the fire.

'Yes, ma'am . . . just a little bit,' Montgomery replied with the air of a guilty, but impish child about him.

'Look, Monty, make use of the room whilst we have Beth dry your clothes off properly, then eat and you can be on your way again. I shall give you the alms needed for the family you told me about earlier and all shall be well with you.' He winked at Montgomery who was grateful for his friend's ingenuity and tactfulness.

'Thank you. You are more than kind, Douglas.' He smiled at Leticia.

'If you stay in the room I shall have some food brought to you, and your clothes, as soon as Biddy has dried them,' Leticia told him and Montgomery knew it was as an order to be obeyed as much as an offer of help. Douglas had a formidable wife, but he appeared to love her for all her unyielding nature.

Montgomery was glad to be able to shed the cold damp clothes and crawl into a fresh bed in his oversized shirt. It was coarser than he was used to, but he was grateful for the kindness and help he had received from the young woman.

He would have to return to Moorsham Place and sort out his current situation, and then he would pay the lady a proper visit and repay her kindness. Douglas appeared in the doorway; he had Beth remove the folded garments that Monty had left outside of the door.

'So my fortunate friend, how did you come to be captured? And more amazingly how did you escape?' Douglas sat on the side of the bed.

'Someone knew where the meeting was to be. The old cruck barn had been surrounded by a press gang of about twelve men. They were armed with pistol and clubs and had chains ready. There was no sign of them, they had bedded in and waited motionless until we arrived.

'It was well-planned and we walked into the spider's web like unsuspecting flies.' Montgomery stared at his friend. He was still annoyed that he had not seen or smelt the trap.

'However did you escape?' Douglas asked. 'Surely you could not break manacles and collars.'

'Of course not, but that is the reason I believe that we were set up. They were well organised regarding our capture, but then were so boastful about how easy their prey had been caught this time that they became careless and the guards started to drink. So sure that there was nothing we could do, they ignored us completely, so we waited till they fell into a drunken stupor.

'It is a shame that I could not have seen the guards faces when they themselves awoke chained like animals.' Montgomery grinned, but noticed Douglas was looking most severe. He did not share the same humour in such matters, Montgomery thought.

'Well it is fortunate indeed that you are free once more or who knows what sea you would have ended up sailing,' Douglas said as he rose. 'I'll have your tray sent to you.'

'Thank you, Douglas.' Montgomery then added, 'I will repay you with interest.'

'I know that, you have no need to say it. I trust you.' He smiled and left.

Montgomery stared out of the window towards the distance and felt uneasy, but he couldn't put his finger on what it was other than he felt that somewhere in everything that had happened he had missed something. What? He didn't know other than the infuriating feeling that it should be obvious . . . but it wasn't.

A young maid brought in a tray for him. He was standing staring into oblivion by the window when she entered. His hands were placed firmly on his hips, as he recalled every detail of what had happened to him within the last forty-eight hours.

The long shirt of Maggie's father hung over him like a nightshirt. He heard a stifled giggle and as he turned he realised he was standing there in only a stranger's coarse shirt.

'Beth, return to the kitchen immediately!' The maid's face changed from geniality to one of shame as Leticia's voice reprimanded her. 'I will thank you not to display your body in such a way in front of an innocent girl, sir. Think of my husband's position if not that of your own!'

She stared at him and he was not only uncomfortable at receiving such a curt reprimand whilst being a guest in his friend's house, but also at the thinly-disguised loathing he sensed from this most uncompromising of women. How different she was from the young woman, Maggie Chase.

'I apologise, I was admiring the view and did not stop to think.' He pointed to the window.

'Obviously, but the girl was! When one is partially attired one should think even more.' The woman stormed out of the room shutting the door firmly behind her.

How very different, he mused, one associate has a heart of stone, the other, a total stranger, has a heart that overflows with compassion.

8

Maggie knocked on the old door and waited whilst Hester opened it wide. The short stout figure appeared. With a white lace bonnet immaculately placed over her greying hair, she looked at Maggie through grey eyes. Clasping her hands in front of her she raised her chin in the air. 'Miss Chase, what a surprise this is. I was not expecting to see you so soon, how pleasant.'

'I hope you don't mind my calling on you unannounced, it was just that I was doing some baking Mrs . . . ' Maggie blushed slightly and raised her basket up to show the woman her excuse for her impromptu visit.

'Hester, you may call me Hester, dear.' The woman almost smiled, the wrinkles around her mouth stretched to smooth skin as the downward curve of her lips straightened to a fine line.

'Thank you, Hester. You must call me Maggie also. I was baking and wondered if you would like some of my freshly made scones.' Maggie offered the basket to her.

'Please come in, Maggie. I'm sure we can talk in more comfort in my parlour, and find some privacy too.' The woman stared at two figures approaching the front of the cottage.

Maggie had been expecting a frosty welcome at best, not this open, friendly one that had placed them on first-name terms. It had almost wrong-footed her as none of her previously rehearsed responses seemed relevant anymore.

Maggie kicked the sand from her boots outside the cottage before setting a foot inside. It was impossible with the wind and the dry fine sand for these town cottages to keep it completely from their threshold but it was always polite to try. The two approaching fisherwomen shouted a greeting to Hester.

'Sorry loves, can't chatter now, have

got a visitor. She waved a hand at them and ushered Maggie inside. Hester's reply was said in a jovial manner, but it was equally dismissive in manner. Then she muttered something to herself as she led Maggie inside.

'Sorry . . . Hester, did you say something to me?' Maggie asked not knowing if she had been expected to reply.

'No dear, I was just musing over what a pair of nosey bodies Lizzie and Dylis Bramble are. Your presence here has now been noted and will be around the town before we sip our first cup of tea.' Hester pointed to a rocking chair by the fire. A soft cushion lay upon it and a lace cover decorated its back. 'You will stay and have a drink with me, won't you, Maggie Chase?'

Maggie looked at the craftsmanship of the lace. 'This is beautiful, did you make it, Hester?'

'Yes, I did, but it is meant to be used not admired so please sit your body down, make yourself at home and share a drink with me.' Hester's voice was filled with a tone of authority.

'Yes, of course I will. Sorry, it is just I have not seen work so fine other than that of my own mother's.' Maggie sat down and watched the older lady remove two pretty cups from her cupboard. She placed them on a small table and set to making a pot of tea.

She fidgeted nervously with her skirt as Hester poured the welcome drink out. Maggie's attention was taken by a spy glass, a long one that hung from a hook against the wall. She had seen Captains with them for spotting far off ships' colours, but not hung on a cottage wall. She wondered if Hester had been left it by a brother in the navy or if it was a gift from a lost love.

'So tell me, Maggie Chase, what has really brought you to my door?' The same grey eyes that had welcomed her in such a friendly manner now stared at her directly.

Maggie returned her gaze, straight into the woman's bright astute eyes and could not help but stifle a grin. 'Am I really that transparent, Hester?' Maggie asked, and was surprised when the woman shook her head, the white bonnet on her head flopping this way and that as she moved.

'Not at all, you did very well, miss. However, I am old enough to sniff out a subtle softener a mile off. So what is it you really want from me? Or what is it that you want to know? And has the Reverend's good wife sent you here, because if she has, you can take those scones . . . ?'

'No, no, nothing like that at all. I don't know her, except to greet in church and, to tell you the truth, with the way she looks down her nose at me I don't really wish to. I was walking along the road when the Reverend Higgs passed me in his gig. He stopped and offered me a lift to your door. I was coming here because I wanted to talk to you about a school for the villagers' children.

'I was hoping to teach the children to

read and write, but perhaps I should talk to the townsfolk first directly rather than make any arrangements myself. What would you suggest I do?' Maggie took the fine porcelain cup that had been offered to her and sipped the tea. It was good, not a rough or cheap blend.

Maggie knew the difference because of the various types her father had brought back with him.

'I suggest, with all due respect, that you let the youngsters learn to fish and gut and do what their parents before them did, then they will be able to feed themselves and shall survive. No good giving them ideas above what they are called to do in this world. That leads to trouble and there is enough of that about in these parts nowadays. I can tell you.' Hester gulped a mouthful of her drink, then as if remembering her manners, dabbed her lips delicately with a kerchief.

'But that is my point, Hester, they will learn to survive, but what about the quality of their lives. What will happen when the new road is finished? Their expectations should be going up, their children will be exposed to more of the world than they have ever known. More than this stretch of coast or the whaling fleets of Whitby.

'Strangers will come here, with new businesses and the town will grow. Are all the townsfolk only good enough to be fishermen and women? What about the jobs that will come with the trade? Anyone who knows their letters and can count and account will have a better standard of living. Surely they deserve a chance to expand their own town, their own way?' Maggie stopped to sip her tea remembering what the Reverend had said about her passion and tempering it with wisdom.

9

'Tell me, Maggie Chase, why should you care? This is not your hometown. You weren't born among us. So what are these people to you?' Hester tilted her head slightly and stared at her with a look of genuine puzzlement.

'They are my neighbours, Hester . . . and besides that, I think that the children deserve a better start in life even if their parents can't see it for themselves,' Maggie looked into the fire. ' . . . and I don't know how to be a fisher-wife, I have an education and at least I can share that.'

'Well, that is a more honest and convincing answer than the 'Lady Leticia' gave me before I showed her the door.' Hester chuckled and hugged herself as she rocked backwards in her chair.

'Who is the Lady Leticia?' Maggie

asked innocently, not realising it was the Reverend's wife that Hester referred to.

'Leticia Higgs, Maggie, is someone who thinks her body everyself.' Hester laughed at the confused expression on Maggie's face. 'Don't worry, girl, it's only a local expression. It means the woman's a stuck up bit who deserves to be brought down a peg or two. What concerns me most though, is how you would cope with your new 'venture' without your worldlier mother.'

'I can teach. I love teaching and I love children also,' Maggie said with enthusiasm, although the reference to her mother did lower her confidence, but she tried not to let it show.

'Oh, I don't doubt that, but how do you convince them,' she pointed to the door, 'that you are 'worthy and able' to teach them? Or that they needed to be taught?' Hester folded her arms and looked pointedly at Maggie.

'Well, I thought that you could

possibly help me there. I am somewhat at a loss as to know where to start with them.' Maggie needed this woman's blessing. Without her approval there would be no school, or rather, no people to teach. 'Had my mother already spoken to you about this?' Maggie had not realised that her plans may have already been discussed.

'Yes, but not as you suspect. She never came here. Initially she had spoken to Letty Higgs in order to air her idea. Higgs commended the idea as a project she was already instigating. She would organise a room, tables and chairs and would run the school as a cross between a Dame School and poorhouse, with her puritanical figure as the matriarch. Your mother's idea, like your own was more realistic and enthusiastic. You wanted to teach the locals not preach to them.

'Then of course your poor ma became ill. I sat with her for you on a couple of occasions, as you know, and she discussed her ideas at length with me. I agree with the both of you,' Hester let out a long slow breath, 'but I am not your mother and did not wish to be, she has gone.'

'I have no wish for you to be either. No-one can replace her. I want to do this in my own right.' Maggie's answer was charged with indignation. 'No offence intended.'

'None taken, lass. But it is as well to clear the air now. You have two things in your favour. Firstly, you are honest and that bodes well with me because I have no time for two faced never-you-minds, and secondly, you've got your fill of common sense, because without me to guide you, you'll fail and you know it too.'

Hester nestled back in her chair and relaxed her arms. Her smile broadened lifting the corners of her mouth fully upwards. 'So how do you intend these poor people to pay for your teaching, girl, or are you doing this for the good of your Christian conscience?'

'Not quite, although I would teach

the poorest for nothing, but perhaps a little chore or a piece of work in exchange for my time would work. I need food, and things like any other. Those that can pay for proper lessons will pay for them in the morning. The afternoon I can teach smaller groups to fit around their work and then they can pay in kind.'

'You need me to tell you who could pay what, amongst them,' Hester said thoughtfully.

'So you will help me to persuade the people?' Maggie asked, and leaned forward.

'You may find yourself with an enemy amongst our newer more affluent townsfolk.'

'Surely not Mrs Higgs. Her husband is so pleasant. Should I speak with them to smooth the way, whilst you talk to the people? You will won't you?' Maggie persisted.

'You're drinking my tea, aren't you?' Hester asked.

'Yes,' Maggie answered.

'Then what do you think?' Hester answered.

'Yes, you will,' Maggie said with enthusiasm.

'Yes!' Hester said, and watched as Maggie sat back relaxed in the chair and finished her tea. 'But you'll find that your pleasant Reverend will bully you, girl, into letting Mrs Higgs be your own matriarch. I say we talk first, decide numbers, times, basics needed and then we shall both go together to see them.'

'Do you think that would be wise, Hester?' Maggie asked.

'Don't patronise me! I can hold my own with the best of them. I wasn't dragged up on the beach like some of them and I can read and write as well as you — plus a smidgeon of Latin!' Hester rounded.

'How? I mean, why haven't you started a school of your own before now, then?'

Maggie was not quite as surprised as Hester had expected because the accent that Hester used with the townsfolk had drifted away when they spoke on their own. There was obviously more to her than she liked people to see.

'My father was a learned man who discovered a liking for liquor when my mother passed on. It was both his and my ruin.' Hester sniffed the air and looked to the fire, then her face hardened as suddenly as it had softened. 'So what happens when your father returns?'

'We have not heard from him for nearly a year. I don't even know if he is still alive. He will have to accept what has been happening here when or if he does return.'

Hester seemed to accept this answer. 'Now, miss, you already know more about me than most in this village, so tell me, *partner*, who was the young man who crept out of your cottage in the early hours of this morning?'

Maggie nearly dropped the cup.

'Oi! That's me best china. First rule of any friendship, Maggie is trust and honesty.' She took the cup from a shocked Maggie. 'I've been honest with you so tell Hester all about him or it will be around the town by nightfall.'

The line of Hester's mouth set firmly again and Maggie knew there would be no good denying the man had been there.

Maggie saw the glint in Hester's eyes and realised that this lady had earned the reputation that went before her. Her attention wandered back to the spy glass which was hanging on the wall and Maggie realised that this cottage had the best vantage point of any in the village.

With that she could see beyond the town to her own cottage on the edge of the wooded gill. Even on a clear moonlight night she would be able to see a figure running across the open moor behind her cottage.

'There isn't much that I miss, but I insist on complete trust amongst my friends.' Hester leaned forward. 'We are to be friends.'

'I can't tell you much about him, Hester. He had escaped from the press gang and I helped him to hide instead of being recaptured and that is all there is to tell. They were chasing him and I couldn't bear the thought that they would hurt him again,' Maggie explained. 'He had already had a beating at their hands, and had a wound on his arm.'

'Girl, you have to toughen up. You're too soft for this world.' Hester shook her head.

'What would you have done?' Maggie asked, and Hester looked quite taken aback.

'Helped him, I suppose.'

'Then perhaps we are not so different,' Maggie replied.

Hester laughed, 'Perhaps not.'

10

It was with a sense of relief that when the bedroom door opened, it was Douglas who brought Montgomery his dry clothes. 'There you are Monty.' He placed them down on the bed and looked at his friend, somewhat sheepishly. 'Leticia has certain standards, Monty. I don't think she meant to offend you, just remind you of the position we are in here. You know loose tongues love to wag . . . reputations. I am truly sorry if you have been offended in any way.'

His friend spoke in a lowered voice from behind the firmly closed door.

'Don't worry, Douglas, after the beating I received the other night a lashing from your wife's tongue does nothing but bruise the old ego, and that, as we all know, can be a good thing,' Montgomery answered diplomatically, although his thoughts were focused on leaving as soon as he could.

'That's the spirit!' Douglas said, and sat down on the window seat whilst Montgomery dressed. 'So what do you intend to do now?'

'Leave, Douglas, and start my quest all over again.' Montgomery fastened his jacket.

'Why don't you return home? Go and see your father, explain to him what is happening to you. Why you feel the way you do and listen to his point of view — be his right hand man. You know it is what he wants. Believe me, if he finds out who you have been mixing with you will wish you had been put on that ship.' Douglas waved a warning finger at him.

'No, I will not do that because he will not see reason. He sees only his way and no other. He is . . . '

'Stubborn,' Douglas added.

'Yes! See, you say it yourself.'

'Like his son,' he added and stared accusingly at Montgomery who glared back defiantly and did not want to back down. He had the right of the matter on his side. Being a son did not mean he had to be as his father. He could be his own man, with his own ideals, and his involved more than the profit on a page.

'I am determined, Douglas, that Father will listen to the voice of reason before these people, hardened by their poverty, take matters into their own hands. I want to find out how deep and wide-spread the mutinous talk is. Then Father will have to listen to me, or his mills will be under attack. I believe these men are sufficiently organised to cause a revolution, Douglas.'

Montgomery stared at the man seated opposite him.

'Then God bless you because, I believe, you are on a fool's mission. If the rabble-rousers don't find out who you are and attack you, then your father might and he will disinherit you. You are being naïve at best or an idiot at worst. Either way, you cannot win, my friend.' Douglas stood up and patted his back. He handed him a pouch from his pocket and said, 'Return it, if and when you can.'

Montgomery took it with some reluctance. 'I shall repay this, with interest to you as soon as I am able . . . have faith.'

Douglas laughed. 'I do. But place yours in God, not man. I've made enquiries, Monty, and the press gang has long since gone. They went down towards Baytown and took a thrashing from the locals from what I heard; went away with their tails between their legs.'

'Thank you, Douglas. I shall consider your advice . . . '

'And ignore it,' Douglas added.

'And decide what would be the best course of action for me to take next.' Montgomery walked to the door. He thanked Leticia from the doorway of the parlour, for her kindness. She looked up momentarily from her embroidery and nodded, rather stiffly, in return.

'What do I tell your father when I see

him next week, Montgomery?' Douglas asked, as Monty stepped out into the bracing sea air.

'Say nothing, unless he specifically asks you if you have seen me. Then, of course, I would not expect you to lie, but I would prefer that this matter was left as an issue for us to resolve when the time is right.'

'Then I shall pray that the time of reconciliation will be soon.' Douglas looked imploringly at him but Monty turned his head away.

'You do that.' Monty shook his friend's hand and left, walking down the sandy road into town. It would make life easier if it turned out that one of the locals was there last night, but although he doubted it, he knew he had to start somewhere. Besides, he needed to think through what Douglas had said to him.

Heads turned and eyes stared at the stranger as he walked past the fishing cobles that were lined up along the sandy beach opposite the row of cottages and the cluster of shops.

Smoke swirled up from the bakery in the centre of town, fishing nets, lobster and crab pots were stacked high between the cobles and at the end of the higgledy-piggledy row the inn had pride of place. It was one of the few buildings that stood three floors high.

A board with a black swan, swayed in front of it in the wind. He braced himself against the gusts and headed straight for it. Perhaps there, he would find one of the local men who had decided to take the law into their own hands.

* * *

Maggie left the warmth and shelter of Hester's cottage in high spirits. They had arranged to meet at church the following Sunday and they would approach Leticia and her group of respectable town's folk, hopefully arranging a meeting to discuss the opening of a school, mainly for the children but open to offer lessons to adults who showed an interest in learning.

Maggie entered the bakery; the heat met her at the door as did the portly figure of Martha Hood. 'Have you heard the news, Miss Chase?'

The high-pitched tone of Martha's voice was filled with excitement. She was rubbing her floury hands against her apron.

'No, Mrs Hood. I have heard nothing of great interest.' Maggie looked up as Lizzie Ketch entered the bakery from the back store room.

'You mean Hester hasn't heard yet, either? Now that's a first!' She sat down on a stool in the corner of the small cottage and started to bite into a pie. Her bony fingers and long angular face were in stark contrast to her companion, Martha, who owned the bakery.

'Will someone tell me what it is that is so intriguing?' Maggie asked.

'There's been a press gang around these parts, and men were took, but they escaped and poor Reverend Kemp, he got in their path and, well, he were beaten up, and 'as just been found behind the old inn. There's a stranger roamin' around the town and 'e's been chased up on to the moor.

'All the men — well, except those who are out at sea, are hunting him. You best stay down here, lass. You don't want to be out on your own with a murderer on the loose, now do you?' Martha looked at her.

'I thought you said that Mr Theodore was beaten not murdered?' Maggie asked.

'Well, he would have been murdered if they hadn't chased off the stranger.'

'Aye,' interrupted Lizzie, 'Ready to plant the last killing blow, I bet.'

'I'd best be telling Hester. She lives on the edge of town. I'll go straight back there,' Maggie turned to leave.

'Here,' Martha shouted to her. 'Take this with you.' She tossed her a loaf and Maggie gratefully put it into her bag.

'Yer can pay for it next time yer in!' Lizzie added.

'I can pay for it now,' Maggie said defensively.

'Oh go on with yer, lass,' Martha said waving her hand at her. 'Ignore the miserly old basket.'

'Miserly, no wonder you is poor, Martha . . . '

'It's you eatin' me out of house and home that's taking my profits not one loaf, yer old trout.'

'Trout is it?'

Maggie left the two to enjoy their sparring match for their rows were legend in the town but they always ended laughing and obviously enjoyed them.

Her mind was in a spin, because, she reasoned that the stranger must be Montgomery, but she couldn't or wouldn't believe that he would attack a curate. Perhaps he was trying to help him? He was seen.

She had to tell Hester, and then return to her cottage. Hopefully, he would think of it as a place of safety. She would help him again, if she could.

The locals were good hardworking people, but they were also hard, and not beyond taking the law into their own hands. Montgomery would not stand a chance against an angry mob.

She knocked frantically on Hester's door. It opened an inch, but no more, 'Hester, there is an attacker on the loose and you must stay inside your cottage, I'm returning to mine now, I . . . ' Maggie stopped mid sentence as Hester's hand grabbed her arm and pulled her inside.

'Stop blithering on my doorstep, lass.' Hester stood with her hands firmly planted on her hips.

'I must get back to my cottage. I have to make sure it is safe,' Maggie answered and put her hand on the door handle.

Hester was pulling an old cloak around her and unhooked the spyglass from its place on the wall.

'What are you doing?' Maggie asked.

'Coming with you! You see, he's already up there.' Hester looked directly into Maggie's eyes. 'You're not going anywhere on your own. You obviously trust this man, but I don't trust anyone until I've met them.' She placed a pistol inside her cloak. 'We shall go together, safety in numbers and we will then decide his fate.'

Maggie opened her mouth to protest but Hester put her hand to the young woman's lips. 'Partners need to trust each other.'

Maggie nodded and wondered if Hester had confused the meaning of the word *trust* with the word *obey*.

11

Montgomery hid in the bushes outside Maggie's cottage. Once satisfied that he had not been followed, he ran across the open ground and hoped the door would be unlocked. It moved easily, 'Miss Chase!' he shouted twice, but there was no reply.

He stepped inside and closed the door. The fire glowed, burning low in the hearth. He added more wood and stoked it until it breathed new heat and life into the room. He hoped the young woman would not be gone long, he needed her help and felt the time had come for him to be honest with her.

Whoever had attacked Theodore had left him in a bad way. Montgomery wished he had arrived a few moments earlier because then he might have been able to stop his friend from getting a good beating.

Theodore would have been able to tell them all who had attacked him, and Montgomery would not now be running away as an outlaw for the second time in as many days. But who would do such a thing to a priest?

No wonder he could not convince anyone to believe him when he said he was trying to help the man. It must have looked as if he had been caught red-handed trying to murder him. What a mess, Montgomery thought to himself.

He sat down and stared at the flames. Why would anyone attack Theodore of all people? He had obviously stumbled across someone unexpectedly, but whom? And what were they all doing there?

His mind was racing. Now, how would he contact the disbanded men? Unless it was them who had attacked Theodore, in which case it would make more sense for him to return to his father and talk directly to him.

He had failed in his own plan to change the course of a group of rebels and save his own world from chaos. Dreams that he had had of striking a peace between two warring sides had been smashed, like the mills in the nearby towns.

He sank his head into his hands, rubbing his eyes. He had to return to his home town and take up his rightful place. He was lost here. Montgomery realised his own arrogance was the making of his downfall. Montgomery heard the door open behind him.

He turned around, straightening his back and holding his head high as he had been brought up to appear, proud, strong and masculine, not wanting to seem beaten in any way. He was expecting to see the beautiful face of his new friend, Maggie. Instead, he saw a pistol with its barrel aimed at his head. The woman holding it was mature in years, but her eyes were hard like the features of her weather-worn face.

'Now, before you do anything hasty, ma'am, may I explain that I am a friend of the owner of this cottage.' He slowly stood up to his full height.

'Sit back down, mister,' Hester snapped out the command angrily. 'So you know Ezekiel Chase, do you?'

Montgomery sat down and smiled his most charming smile; at least, he sincerely hoped it was. 'Not exactly. However, I am an acquaintance of his daughter, Miss Margaret Chase. I'm sure if she were here she would dispense your concern, ma'am.'

'Oh, she would, would she?' Hester stepped aside so that Maggie's figure was then within Montgomery's line of vision.

Maggie looked at the pale face of this tired, hunted man and closed the door firmly behind her forcing across the bolt to secure it.

'Yes, I would,' she answered, 'but I'm not sure that I should or why, for that matter, but Hester, he does need our help.' Maggie looked at the older woman imploringly.

'Oh, on that I would agree with you or he would be dead meat by now, but you, sir, are going to explain yourself fully, or I'll call in the mob and this chit of a gullible lass won't be able to stop me.' Hester sat down at the table still holding the pistol firmly trained on Montgomery. 'Now, start talking, and don't give me any flimsy lies or my finger just might slip.'

'Montgomery, you can trust Hester. But we need to be able to trust you and up to now you have been chased by His Majesty's navy and the townsfolk. Tell us what happened to Theodore and what is going on here.'

Maggie looked at his tired sad eyes and felt her heart sympathise with him. But she knew Hester was right. Her heart was ruling her head as she felt strangely drawn to this handsome looking man. She could tell by his hands that he was not used to heavy work and by his manner and stature that he was not used to servitude, but he was vulnerable and a mystery.

'I wanted to help the people who have been planning to attack mills within this region, but it has all gone terribly wrong and I don't want Theodore or you hurt by my actions.'

Montgomery was looking straight at Maggie whose attention hung on his every word. Hester listened but watched unmoved.

'Very noble,' Hester said, 'now this time start at the beginning. Lass, make a drink, I think we may be here for a long time.'

Maggie filled up the kettle that hung over the fire. She looked at Montgomery as she stood beside him. 'What is your full name?'

'Montgomery Fulton Mudford. My father owns four woollen mills over thirty miles west of here. There has been trouble amongst the workforce. Other mills both to the north and south of us are having similar problems. One was even burned to the ground.

'My father and two other prominent owners are talking of bringing in the dragoons to sort the troublemakers out. They are angry and will not listen to the reasons for the people's militant actions . . . they want to see the leaders hung as an example to the rest.'

'That's all very interesting, but tell me what you expected to achieve here?' Hester persisted.

'I was working with Douglas's brother, Brian — Reverend Higgs, that is, who is our local priest. We thought that if I could infiltrate the meeting, raise a petition and place it before my father and his friends then we could act as negotiators and avoid the needless loss of life. He had heard from a frightened wife of one of them that they were planning this meeting here.

'I was told the secret sign, and where to meet, then shown to the place. However, others had their own plans and it was an ambush. The rest you know.'

He looked up at Maggie. 'I am truly sorry to have involved you in my foolishness. I realise now that these people are so angry, they may well have lynched me before I had the chance to explain my intended purpose.'

'So what happened to Reverend Theodore?' Hester asked.

'That I do not know or understand. He was aware of my plan, as was Douglas. I was sent an introductory note by Brian and stayed here, unseen, for two days whilst they told me a little of this place. I can't imagine who would wish to silence him or why.' Montgomery looked most concerned.

'So what do you think you will do now?' Hester still had the pistol trained on him. She had not lowered her guard since entering the cottage. Maggie poured them all a drink.

'I need to return home. It is vital I speak to my father, who thinks I am in London visiting friends, and explain what has been happening here. He must listen to some of the people's concerns and act on them or there will be an uprising. I'm sure no one would gain from that.'

'Why do you care? The less the folks have, the more money lines your family's pockets.' Hester's words were edged with bitterness. 'Why aren't you protecting your inheritance?'

'Yes, that's true, but we have more than enough money and I believe it is time to give something back to the people who have worked to build up Father's empire.' Montgomery spoke with the passion of sincerity and Maggie could not help but admire him for having the courage to try and resolve the situation in his own way. Surely, he was not only risking his father's wrath but his life too.

'You, sire,' Hester said, 'are an idealistic fool!'

'Hester!' Maggie rebuked her. 'He is very brave!'

Hester's eyes rolled upwards and she shook her head.

'He is a blithering idiot.' She turned to face Montgomery. 'You are ignorant of the people you want to help and have little common sense to guard you against the reality of life out there without your rank in society to protect you.'

She looked from Montgomery to Maggie and laughed, then placed the pistol down on the table. She lifted her cup to her lips and sipped it delicately.

'You make a fine pair. One thinks he can stop a rebellion single-handedly, the other wants to teach them to read and write! I would say you two have restored my belief in human kindness, if it wasn't for your stupidity.'

Maggie and Montgomery both blushed slightly and looked at each other before grinning broadly. There was a truth in the old woman's words that they could not deny, but they also were both acknowledging the fact that they liked the idea of making a fine pair.

'So will you help us, Hester?' Maggie asked.

Hester looked at Montgomery and raised an eyebrow.

'I think, ma'am, we could both do with the benefit of your more worldly knowledge in extricating us from our current dilemma.' Montgomery's words were filled with an air of sarcasm, but then he lowered his voice and very simply added, 'Please.'

'I'll help you find out who decided to attack a priest, and God help him, we'll bring the vermin to justice. I'll also help you to hide until we can get you back to where you belong, which is Pelham Hall, I presume, near Beckton Bridge?'

'You know it?' Montgomery was obviously surprised.

'Oh yes, I know of your family and of the money you have built up in one short generation. So when I have helped you out of your own mess, sir, you can help this girl by placing some of that gold from your family's pockets into our school and pay the working people back. That way, you will help the ones who want to help themselves and stay away from troublemakers.

'If an uprising happens, it happens, and that is beyond both you and me, but I will help you — this time. But listen to me, young man. I am not just a sweet old lady . . . '

Montgomery grinned, but one stare

from Hester and a glance at the pistol, and he resumed a serious composure.

'I have friends. You double-cross these people or this young lass, for that matter, and there will be nowhere you can hide north of the Humber. Do we understand each other?'

'Yes, perfectly, but I won't, I am a man of honour.' Montgomery looked at Maggie.

'Oh, don't waste your time trying to persuade her, she's already deeply sunk in your helpless pup charm. Now, what did you see when you found Theodore? Did he say anything to you?'

'His eyes were shut, he was asking for Douglas. I told him I would take him to him, but he grabbed hold of my arm by the gash and I dropped him. I was still holding on with one hand when the cry went up and they came at me with fish knives. I ran for it. I now know what a fox feels like for I have been hunted to ground. It was only because I managed to double back through the marram grass that I made my way down to the gill and retraced my steps back here. They thought I had headed for the moor road.'

'So you didn't see anyone else?' The woman stood up. 'I'm leaving you here, together.' Hester took her pistol and unbolted the door. 'Lay one hand on her, man, and I'll make sure they catch you!'

'I am a gentleman!' Montgomery said defiantly.

'Aye, that's what worries me. You're most likely used to having or taking what you want.' She stared at Maggie. 'You remember your mother was a respectable lady, don't let her or yourself down.'

'Hester!' Maggie's cheeks burned with embarrassment, but Hester just wagged a warning finger at her.

'I'll be back before dark . . . to stay. Don't leave, either of you.' She opened the door and left.

The two young people stared at each other. Uneasiness filled the air.

'I won't . . . ' Montgomery began as

he moved closer to Maggie.

'I know,' she said, as she stroked his arm in a caring natural manner. He in turn rubbed his hand against her shoulder.

'I owe you a great deal. Thank you, you are the most beautiful and kind person I have met for a long time.'

She leaned in to him and his arm held her close.

'Maggie,' he said, the word flowing softly from his mouth. She liked the sound on his lips.

'Yes,' she answered and tilted her head up to his. The kiss that greeted it felt as natural as it was consuming. They embraced for what seemed like minutes of bliss, taking her away from her loneliness and into the warm caress of another human being.

It was only the pounding on the door that separated them. 'Hide in the dairy cupboard, quickly!'

Maggie waited until he was out of sight before opening the door.

12

'Maggie Chase!' a deep voice bellowed out as a heavy fist pounded upon the wood. Maggie waited until all trace of Montgomery was out of sight before she dared to open the door.

Maggie thought that it must be the search party. Perhaps, she thought, Hester was not the only one to see him run to her cottage. Normally, her home was open to the few visitors who made their way up to the headland.

She took in a deep intake of breath and unbolted the door, then stepped back in total shock. Her body froze to the spot, unable to move, of all the people and of all the times he had chosen to return now. A bearded figure towered over her as he stepped inside into the warmth of the cottage. The naval sack was unmistakable, the captain's hat and coat the same.

She stared at him and her mouth dropped open, but no words left her lips. After a moment she heard a small voice speak, then Maggie realised it was her own. 'Father!'

'Is that any way to greet me? Give me a hug, lass. It's been quite a while this time.' He held her tightly, squeezing out her last breath before releasing her just as quickly. That was all the affection she would expect of him until he repeated the same gesture before leaving her again.

She did as he bid her. Her arms had been barely able to reach around his girth. He smelt of salt sea air, his beard was wild and in need of a trim, the tanned lined skin above it all gave away his years at sea. He threw his bag inside and walked over to the fire.

Maggie just stared at him, unable to move. Usually her mother would have had a drink in his hand and a plate on the table the minute she saw him return. Maggie would watch and listen as an outsider, but now there was just her father and her and she faced him, wondering how they would ever be able to converse one to one.

Then she remembered Montgomery hidden in the dairy cupboard and her stomach seemed to take on a life of its own. She swallowed and offered him a drink, forcing herself to move. Closing the outside door she moved over between him and the passage.

'Now, lass. I came back as soon as I could, once I received your letter about poor Cecily. I'm really sorry, Maggie, that you were left to fend for yourself. I see you've been doing fine, but I've come back now to sort things out. It's time you were left in a proper house, but your Ma, bless your soul, would never be parted from you so up here you stayed.'

Maggie poured her father a drink and fetched him some ham, cheese and her fresh scones. 'It's really fine here, Father. I have plans for the future. I will be able to fend for myself. I shall . . . '

'What talk is this? You're a child, lass.'

He placed a whole scone into his mouth and chewed, spitting out crumbs as he spoke.

'You shouldn't be providing for yourself, you shall be wed. I've some ship mates, young, strong and one is another captain's son who will be glad to have a fine lass like you for a wife. No, you're coming back with me. You should have been having children of your own. Best to start young then you are more likely to have ones that'll survive to adulthood.

'We'll take a ship from Whitby to London and whichever one of the lads puts up the best offer, and of course that you can abide, you shall have as your husband. Then, once the ceremony is all done with, you can sail with me to the East. I aim to set up store there.'

He smiled up at her revealing, discoloured, uneven teeth beneath the matted hair.

'Am I to have no say in this at all?' Maggie asked. Her fists clenched tightly within the folds of her skirt. She could feel her cheeks burning.

'I told you, you can pick the one that suits you best once I've narrowed them down to the few I'll consider acceptable. I'm after a partner in me business too, so don't you go getting all selfish on me!' He shook his head. 'It were a good enough arrangement for yer Ma, so it will do for you.'

'I am opening a school here with Hester, in the town. We have made plans and it will help the village.' Maggie stared at him. He was big, brusque and frightening, but she had seen her mother stand up to him and she was determined that she would do the same.

He walked over. Standing square in front of her he stared straight down into her eyes. 'You are not going to be teachin' these miserable folks anythin'. Hester can do it hersel', you are goin' to be a wife — a good and loyal one. You will obey your father and you will pack your things up this night. I will auction off the cottage tomorrow and we will be out of here as soon as the business is done. At least you ain't bein' sold on, by your own husband, like your mother was. You're fresh and you'll get a good deal.'

'What do you mean . . . sold on?' Maggie asked, forgetting that behind a narrow door in the passage a rather uncomfortable Montgomery could hear every word that was spoken.

'Just what I said, but yer fancy Ma never gave you that bit of knowledge, did she? No lass, you came in a job lot. Her husband, a gent by all accounts, hit hard times, so to save his skin from the debtor's prison he took you and her to the market. Don't get me wrong. Me and her had some good times and she was always treat right, but that's the way it is and now you'll sail with me to the Far East and meet me other family, and we shall have a good life. You'll see. Then you can teach yer own kin how to read and write. These blighters are nothin' to yer.'

Maggie was shocked to the core. Her heart pounded deep within her chest. Her beautiful mother, kindly, gentle and intelligent was sold, like a slave, well perhaps not, but auctioned like an animal to this man who had never felt to Maggie like a father in all her years there. Now she knew why. 'Who am I, then. You said we were a job-lot, then if you are not my father, who is?'

'Some man named Bindle, Jeremiah Augustus. Aye, I remember the name well. But as far as the law is concerned you are my daughter, so pack up, shut up your moaning and tomorrow we will try to sell off this place and head south.'

He swung his bag over his shoulder and walked off along the passage.

'Where are you going?' Maggie shouted almost panicking as he stopped next to the diary cupboard.

'To me bed, I'm fair bug . . . tired. I take it you've no objection?' Maggie could not speak as he leaned on the door. 'Good, make me dinner whilst I rest.'

He pulled the trunk from the room and threw the clothes that belonged to her mother over it. You can pack up what you need in there and we'll sell on the rest. Hurry up, lass. I need me kip.'

13

Maggie dragged the clothes and trunk into the parlour. She closed the door behind her and sat in the room. Quickly she put anything she could use or valued into a bag from the cubby hole behind the dresser and waited until she had heard at least ten deep snores.

Then she tiptoed along the corridor to the dairy cupboard, and as quietly as she could, she opened the narrow door.

Montgomery was curled into as small a ball as he could on the cold tiled floor. He crawled out and made his way to the parlour. Maggie had on her mother's cloak, hat and muff.

'I have no time to explain now, but we both must leave this minute!' Maggie said quickly, but could tell by the look of empathy in his deep eyes that he had heard and understood her predicament only too well.

'Leave the bag, I'll see you need for nothing,' Montgomery whispered to her, and put a caring arm around her shoulder.

'But he'll sell them and they were all I have of my mother.' Maggie looked imploringly.

'Then we shall hide them in the woods as we go, but we need all speed as we will have two parties looking for us. I must get back to my father's house. There you will be safe and we can sort out the rights of your paternity from there.'

'You heard,' she said. Her shoulders drooped as she was filled with a sense of shame.

He kissed her cheek. 'I heard that that oaf is not your father, and I am relieved, so now let's go before he awakes and rearranges my skull, shall we?'

Maggie walked out of the cottage with the bag. She ran down the wooded path and into a thicket. There she wedged her precious few belongings behind a rock, within the crevice of the bank. Then, without further words, they ran along the gill towards the old mill at the top, which itself backed on to the moor road.

They sheltered in the old building to catch their breath. Maggie noticed he was staring at her in a most imitate fashion. 'What is it?' she asked.

Without a momentary hesitation, he cupped her face in his hands and kissed her tenderly on the lips.

'Forgive me, Miss Margaret Bindle, but I find you the most lovely, genuine person I have ever met and I want nothing more than to look upon your face for the rest of my days.'

Their eyes were locked upon each others. 'Once you are back amongst society you will view me as a fisher-woman and wonder what madness came over you.'

'Never, I was about to . . . '

'You are about to talk yourself under her skirts and you into the hands of an angry mob. Have you no sense at all, the pair of you?' Hester's angry figure appeared in the open space where once there had been a door to the mill.

'I was being sincere, ma'am. My comments were meant for Maggie alone,' Montgomery answered defensively.

'Perhaps, or perhaps not, but you are not in the correct place or the right time to allow yourself such indulgences. You have to get away from here. Word has it that Captain Chase is back in town.'

'Yes, Hester, he is, and he wants to take me back to London with him and sell up the cottage,' Maggie answered, grateful for the change in conversation.

'Then that explains things.' Hester looked at Montgomery.

'Surely, it was not he who attacked Theodore?' Montgomery asked, and stepped forward as if he were contemplating going back to the cottage to confront him.

'Don't be ridiculous, man. You are no match in your current state for an experienced seaman like him. Theodore has a loose tongue. He means well, but he cost Captain Chase a good deal of money on his last venture. The man had to ditch some cargo at sea before the Revenue Cutter got hold of him. Theodore, the naïve fool had been giving them as much 'helpful' information as he could to keep everyone on the right side of the law.

'He has regained consciousness, but he will not say a word this time about who took a fist to him. He didn't see his attacker. And if you . . . ' she poked Montgomery in the chest, 'had an ounce of sense you would never have told your friend Theodore of your intentions or of the meeting, because when the authorities came calling he had to tell them what he knew.

'You nearly had everyone in the lock-up or on their way out to sea in a man-of-war. Next time you decide to save the workers, think first. You would have been returned in shame to your pa, but the others would have had their time at sea, and who would have fed their families then?'

She shook her head. 'You did more harm than good. So what is your plan for this chit of a lass, because you have ruined her reputation and made her homeless in one day?'

'I have every honourable intention to know Maggie more. I will take her into my care and protection.' Montgomery looked at Maggie and smiled broadly at her. She blushed but returned his smile.

'To what aim?' Hester persisted.

'This is a conversation I should like to have with Maggie privately. It is none of your concern, ma'am.' Montgomery glared at Hester, and Maggie found she could hardly control herself from grinning at the two of them as they stared each other out.

'We really need to be on our way, Hester. I would rather take my chances with Montgomery than be auctioned to the Captain's friend as a wife.' Maggie saw the horror on Hester's face.

‘Is that what he plans?’ she asked incredulously.

‘Yes,’ Maggie answered.

‘Come with me, but stay deathly quiet,’ she turned to Montgomery, ‘and what you are about to see you will forget as fast as you learned of it.’

14

Below the great wheel was the river that fed the creek. Like the mill, it was old, but unlike the mill it still flowed and was a vital part of the local scenery as it twisted its way down from the west.

The huge wheel had been disconnected from the grinding mechanism and had generally fallen into disrepair. They climbed down some rickety wooden stairs to the lower ground level where grain used to be loaded from boats and stored before being refined.

The wooded floor was still sound, though, like most of the building's structure and a few old sacks were still stacked against the wall.

Hester led them outside the building at the water level and told them to keep their backs to the wall of the mill until they were edging along a narrow path by the steep bank of the river.

'Maggie, are you all right?' Montgomery whispered as she stumbled slightly on a loose rock. He received a sharp rap on his arm from Hester. He flinched as it was on his wounded one, but Maggie nodded to let him know that she was fine.

They bent low under the canopy of a willow and Hester stopped by a rocky overhang at the other side of it. The ground was moist here, like walking and slipping on wet clay. Hester leaned in and pulled at a rope that lay under some ferns by their feet. Attached to the other end of it was a coracle.

'Can you use one of these, man?' Hester asked Montgomery.

'I'll soon get the hang of it. I've rowed a boat before, so it can't be that different,' Montgomery said.

'God help you, lass. Be careful not to fidget. You can tip up quite easily.' Hester said quietly as she pulled it around on the water and gave the rope to Montgomery.

He held it firmly. 'Who does it belong to?' he asked.

'Never you mind that! Let's just say it belongs to the community. Now get in and go as far as you can. You best not get caught before you return home. Take care of the lass and remember, sir, you owe this town a school.'

'And a coracle, it now appears,' he answered as he studied the vessel and held the oar that had been wedged firmly into the boat. Montgomery steadied the lightweight craft whilst gingerly Maggie climbed in. then Montgomery followed, giggling like a child on an adventure when he slipped and had to grab for the paddle.

They huddled together in the middle and steadied themselves, then Hester threw the rope at him. Montgomery took the paddle and, as Hester watched them bob off into the river's flow, she was frowning severely at him. He steered it as best he could across the river's breadth and followed its path down stream, away from the creek.

Maggie found it was both frightening, yet exciting. She was so lost in watching every branch and bend as they bobbed along that it was some minutes before either of them spoke. Montgomery had a few near misses with overgrowth and nearly crashed into a rock once or twice until he developed the knack of steering it effectively. But Maggie admired his ability to adapt to every new situation and could see the delight in his eyes as he rose to the challenge of this latest adventure.

They passed by a row of houses, a small hamlet and under a small bridge, apparently unnoticed. Neither spoke as they slipped past.

'I recognise this place. The river will soon flow stronger and grow in width, but we are nearer a town that I recognise and where we will be able to buy a horse to take us to my home.' Montgomery was so excited that he seemed to have forgotten that Maggie would not be going to her home again. She looked away not wanting to show the confusion of emotions that ripped through her.

She missed her mother, loved her own cottage — for that was what she had thought of it as, and felt herself sunk into a mass of self-destructive guilt. She had walked out on the school with Hester instead of fighting for what she and her mother believed in, and she had deserted her father, or the man she had always considered to be him. Now, she had the knowledge that her real father bartered both her and her mother to save his own neck.

'What's wrong? Did you not hear me, Maggie? We will soon be home. Granted I have issues to clear up with my father, but he is a good man, just misguided and slightly stubborn at times. We shall be safe.'

'I understand why you feel happy, Montgomery but I have little to celebrate. I have no home, my plans to fulfil my mother's dream to run a school have been blown away with the wind and the man I thought was my father is . . . nothing to me.'

Maggie looked up into his dark eyes and saw the empathy she craved. If she could have lost herself in his embrace she would have been a willing participant, eager to be swept away by emotion . . . and what she could only define as . . . love.

'You will have a home there — with me. I shall take care of you. I meant what I said to you, Maggie. The school was your mother's dream, not yours. I'm sorry that she didn't live to see it come true, but it would be wrong for you to devote your life to fulfilling someone else's dreams — what of your own, Maggie?'

He steered the coracle over towards the river bank. She held the side of the craft firmly as they bumped their way across the ripples of the water's flow.

'I've never really thought about that, or considered my own. They were always wrapped up with my mother. I loved her very much, you see,' Maggie answered and felt shocked at the admission, as she hadn't.

'Well, it's time that you did, without having feelings of guilt. Regarding that man back there, he has no right to call you his daughter, nor you, your father. If you wish it so, I can help you to trace your natural father.'

'No! That would be worse. Who wants to be reunited with a man who could sell his own wife and child? The notion is intolerable; he should have been arrested.'

Maggie was quite distraught at the thought. The vessel bumped against the bank. Fortunately she needed to use her frustration and anger to haul herself up on to steady and dry land.

15

Montgomery leaped out of the vessel and then carried it up to the tow path. 'Perhaps he was, Maggie. If he gambled his wealth away, he would most likely do the same again with whatever monies he received.'

'Then we were sold for nothing! He'd still end up in jail.' Maggie almost shouted with frustration.

'But at least you two didn't starve and your mother didn't end up a . . . in an even worse situation.' He seemed ill at ease and changed the subject, 'So do you think we should hide or can we sell this?' Montgomery said.

'We can hardly carry it on a horse,' Maggie answered. 'Do you think we'll need it again?'

They made their way to a blacksmith's shop by the river front. Montgomery drove a hard bargain but he came out with coin from the sale and headed straight to a coaching inn on the outside of the town.

There was no chaise or coach available to hire or due until the following day. The only vehicle available for rental was a horse and moorland cart. It would be a slow journey but at least they would be travelling in the right direction, Maggie told herself, realising they would have to sleep in the open country in the wagon.

'Look at it this way . . . ' she said to Montgomery's downcast face. 'We shall have more chance to talk to each other as we travel.' She hoped that would take away the unease they both felt. She smiled at him and he winked back at her, and Hester's words of warning to her about not letting herself or her mother down made her cheeks burn.

Captain Chase woke up in a cold cottage. The man had a sore head, years of heavy drinking had numbed his sense so he rarely awoke feeling as though he was full of life and eager to set sail again, like the young man he had once been.

'Maggie! Maggie!' he waited for a few moments, dozed off again and recalled their previous meeting. Perhaps the lass is sulking because she knew the truth of her past. Well it was about time. He'd been fond of her mother, and she'd not let him down, kept house, cared for him when he was in their home and never questioned him regarding his work or other women. No, she'd been good for him, but that had changed.

His bones didn't like the cold anymore. He yearned for the warmth of the tropics and his Mei, sweet young and eager to please him. No, he would wrap up business here and be gone from these shores within the week. The girl would learn to comply. Her mother had let her have too much of her own head . . . a school indeed! Why did a woman need to learn anything other than to look after their man, house and brats?

No, she had been given ideas well

above her station and he would have one of his friends sort her. He had enough to do, to be bothering with the trifles of a young girl.

'Maggie!' he was losing his patience. He got up and pulled on his coat. He staggered down the passage to the parlour and saw that the fire had burned itself out in the hearth. There was no cot-bed laid out, nor food prepared. In fact there was nothing and no-one there but him. Damn her! She's done a runner.

By hell, he swore that he would find her and drag her back. Where to look? He scratched his head and beard and then a name occurred to him . . . Hester, the busy-body would have a keen idea where she would run. He'd pay the old girl a visit. Captain Chase grabbed a piece of ham and slammed the cottage door behind him as he stormed off towards the town.

16

Captain Chase tore down the path, through the woods and on to the flat sandy beach. He leaned into the strong wind that blew in from the sea, ignoring the fine sand that beat against his face, and crossed over the dunes towards the old town.

He stopped momentarily between two clumps of marram grass atop a dune, seeing the church and vicarage at the end of the main street. Would she go there? He wondered, turning over the possibilities in his mind.

Perhaps she was at the vicarage, but then he could hardly visit them after giving Theodore a thrashing. No, he'd find his answers from the old witch, Hester. She'd filled his girl with notions of schooling the blackguards so, understanding women as he did, he was sure that Maggie would go to a 'mother-hen' figure.

It took him a further twenty minutes before he was positioned in front of Hester's door rapping his fist against it with all his might.

'Quiet!' Hester opened the door only an inch wide. 'What are you trying to do, Chase, break down my door?' Hester was swept aside as he stomped in leaving a sandy trail behind him on her clip rug.

'Where is she?' He turned around accusingly, enraged when there was no sign of his daughter within the cottage. Hester regained her balance and moved slowly to the side, so that her back was leaning against the open door.

'Where is who? You big bully of a man,' she asked, and saw his brow furrow into deep set lines as he scowled at her.

'My daughter! Where is my daughter? You interfering old witch. They'd have burned your type at the stake in the old days. Wastin' her time by fillin' her head with ideas and notions. She ain't from good stock. She isn't goin' to teach in yer school so forget it, woman. She is goin' to wed, and come back with me to the Far East.

'So tell me now, before I break yer skull, where has she gone?' He took a step forward, but Hester pulled her pistol out from her skirt pocket and pointed it at him. She had been expecting a visit from him, that was obvious.

'So, you are not content with beating up a priest but you now want to hit a defenceless old woman,' Hester said, as her thumb rested against the trigger.

'He had a loose mouth, I merely shut it for him.' Chase grinned, then tried to smile at her. 'Look, you know how it is. He blithered, and we can't have that now, can we? Cost me a small fortune on that run.'

'He is a good man. One of honour, a little naïve, but there's no calling for treating a priest like that. It is folly and no good will come of it. Now, get out of my cottage before I call for help.' Hester stepped aside so as to leave a clear pathway to the door for him.

'Who is goin' ter help you against me, woman? Where is my Maggie? I need her today. We have a ship to catch and I don't intend to miss it.' He made no attempt to move.

Hester could see his colour rising in his already ruddy cheeks. 'Then go without her. I don't know where she is, but I hope it is far away from here and you.'

'I'll find her.' He clenched both fists at his sides. 'If you have anything to do with her running away I shall be back here to teach you a lesson about meddling in other folks' business.' The man's voice was bellowing again. With the door open, anyone who passed by could hear, and indeed they had.

Reverend Higgs appeared in the opening. 'I'll take that pistol, Hester. I heard this man confess to attacking poor Theodore. He will not be going on any ship for a long time unless it is to a far off land of His Majesty's choice.'

'What!' Chase exploded into a mad rage. As Hester held out the pistol for the Reverend to take from her, the captain ran at them, knocking Hester and the pistol to the ground and punching the Reverend in the side as he ran down the path and along the beach.

The Reverend Higgs picked up the pistol and let a shot ring out, into the air. Fishermen hauling up their coble from the beach saw the Reverend waving wildly and pointing to Chase as he made for his escape towards the headland and around to the creek's bank.

They gave chase but were quite a distance behind him. He was of heavy frame and laboured hard as he ran. He made his way straight towards the mill, bypassing it along the narrow path. He felt around anxiously for the coracle's rope, but it had gone.

'Damnation!' he swore as the means of his escape had disappeared.

The path beyond narrowed to nothing. Above him the overhang was impassable and too steep to climb. The river at this point was quite deep, so he could not walk across it in safety and he cursed the fact that he couldn't swim. Chase had no choice but to return to the mill and hope he still had time to make it up the bank there to the open moor. His temper burned deeply inside him, but his energy was flagging.

As he retraced his steps to the old mill he heard the voices of his pursuers. He leaned back on to the bank pulling willow branches in front of him. Surely, if they knew the coracle was in use for a drop, then they would not continue, but of course they had no more knowledge than he that it had been Montgomery and Maggie who had used it earlier, so onwards they came.

The first man he knocked into the water, not heeding the man's cry for help as he tried to toss the next after him, but it was Reverend Douglas Higgs, with a reloaded pistol pointed at his face. The sodden man climbed out of the river the other side of him, 'the chase has ended.' The wet man said, grinning broadly at his own joke.

'Bring him.' Higgs backed up the path to the mill. There Chase was bound with a discarded piece of rope. 'You can answer to the authorities for what you have done, man. Theodore will give a full statement and you will not leave these shores for some years to come.'

'No!' Chase shouted, but his pleas were ignored.

17

The drab coloured wagon, covered with a loose canvas cloth pulled out of the town and headed for the moor road that would take Montgomery towards his home. 'It will take us two days to get there, Maggie.'

'Isn't there a shorter cut,' she asked optimistically. 'The old monks' paths, perhaps?' Maggie remembered her mother telling her about how the whole area was criss-crossed by tracks made by monks walking from monastery to monastery in the area.

'I'm afraid not. Not in this old wagon, anyway. We were lucky that he had one that he was prepared to let us use, but it is at the end of its serviceable life. I feel I was taken advantage of in my eagerness to find transport.' Montgomery stared at the old horse pulling them. 'He's due for retirement, too.'

'Are there any inns along the way where we could stop?' She tried to sound as though it was an innocent enquiry, but the idea of spending a night out in the open scared her. However, with the thought of Montgomery next to her, it was a totally different kind of feeling that filled her.

'Maggie, it is better for you if you are not seen travelling alone, unchaperoned, with me. We will try to stay out of people's way. Once we approach the hall, it will not matter anyway, because you are with me. You will be safe then and protected by my good name.'

Maggie smiled to herself as she looked the other way, towards a group of sheep that were eating their fill by the wayside. She liked the sound of being with him and in his protection. She and her mother had survived for years without a man, but it had been a real trial for Maggie since her mother died. At first she had felt vulnerable, scared even, in case a drunken sailor heard she was up there on her own. She shuddered at the thought, and the memory of life on her own.

He placed a comforting arm around her. 'Are you cold?' he asked after she had trembled.

'No — well, just a little, perhaps.' He looked at her, concerned, and held her to him. They plodded on at a pace that was comfortable to the old nag they had purchased. The light started to fade, as evening crept in upon them. Eventually, Montgomery pulled the wagon into the shelter of a small wood.

He unhitched and settled the animal, taking it first to a stream to drink. Maggie helped him to secure the canvas to cut out as much draught as he could, then he laid two blankets on the wagon's floor. They were all that he had been able to afford above the cost of the vehicle itself. 'We have to sleep here tonight, Maggie.' He looked at her and smiled a little sheepishly.

'We can't, Montgomery. It wouldn't be fitting!' Maggie answered, fighting the urge not to protest at all and to do what she wished most, to openly embrace him.

This suggestion, she knew was extremely unwise and presumptuous of him. Her mother would have been disgusted at the thought, but if Maggie was being honest with herself, she wasn't.

'Yes, we do.' He looked at her seriously. 'Look, Maggie, we have to be realistic. Firstly, it will get very cold out here at night so, huddled together, we shall stay warm. Secondly, I shall not insult you or abuse our friendship. Thirdly . . . ' He walked over to her and stroked her cheek tenderly with one finger.

'Thirdly,' she repeated.

'Thirdly, but most important of all, I admire and respect you too much to treat you badly, in any way.' Montgomery meant what he said, Maggie could tell but there was a deep yearning within him — in them both if she was honest, that she sensed whenever they were together. They were drawn to each other, soul mates, was the only way she could think of describing it.

She turned her mouth to his hand and, without thinking, kissed it gently. It was a natural response. He instantly withdrew it, and laughed. 'Oh, Miss Chase, I will need to be strong for us both.' He kissed her forehead and then returned to the wagon, where he had a small packet filled with two bottles of ale, bread and some cheese. It was basic, but it would do for one night at least.

'What is your home like?' Maggie asked, as they ate by a small fire that between them they had managed to build up.

'Quite large, really. There are eight bedrooms, and a landscaped estate surrounding it. Father has worked hard and done extremely well for himself,' Montgomery admitted. 'This is why it is such a shame that he cannot see he could oh so easily lose it just as quickly. But sometimes success blinds a person, distorting their vision. Their values become watered down and thinned as profit raises its ugly power.'

'You sound like Reverend Higgs, Montgomery. His sermons are almost poetic.' She saw him grin at the idea, but it was true. He was a person of passion, and vision also, just like her.

'Yes, I know what you mean because his brother is my dearest friend but I feel, although we were well-meaning in our gesture to solve the problem, we have overstepped our boundaries. Instead of confronting my father, I sought to talk to people I had little knowledge of, and in the process nearly ruined my own life. However,' he winked at her, 'my life has since become entangled with yours.'

'Destiny, fate, whatever you wish to call it, I believe we were meant to cross each other's path,' Maggie said, as he reached out and held her hand in his.

Montgomery kicked out the fire, smothering it with earth, then escorted Maggie to the wagon. 'We shall settle as best as we can and keep warm. You will be safe with me, trust me, Maggie.'

Maggie climbed up into the back and the two snuggled up to each other on the hard wooden floor, wrapping the blanket as tightly around them as they could.

'Are you comfortable?' Montgomery asked.

'No,' Maggie answered honestly. 'Are you?' she asked.

'No,' he replied. Both giggled like nervous children.

'Goodnight,' she said.

'Goodnight,' he replied.

'You're beautiful, Maggie.' His voice was deep and soft the next morning.

Maggie spun around to see him sitting there, staring at her.

He dropped to one knee before her and held her hand. 'I will love you always and want you to feel the same way about me. Marry me, Maggie, and I shall look after you forever.'

There was no humour or casual jocular expression in his manner.

'Are you serious, Montgomery?' she asked him, her head in a whirl of thoughts and emotions. He had never appeared to be more solemn in her presence.

'Absolutely, I've not been more so in my life,' he answered passionately.

'But we hardly know each other.' Her words were uttered before she thought about what she was saying. Both looked into the other's eyes and laughed. 'Are you really sure?'

'You move me in a way that the silly girls at the assembly rooms never have done. Don't doubt my sincerity, Maggie . . . and please do not reject me or I shall be devastated.'

'I accept. How could I not, but what of your father?' Maggie asked.

'He is already married,' he answered and grinned widely.

'You know what I mean.' She stared into his eyes looking for any sign of doubt.

'Let us go and find out, but whatever he feels about any of this, I will have you as my wife so long as you are willing to be.'

18

Theodore awoke in the guest bedchamber of the vicarage. His head ached, his body also, and the room was chilly as Leticia did not approve of too much luxury, like glowing fires. They wasted God's precious gifts to mankind for his comfort rather than his need.

She also believed that the body built up greater resistance to ailments when it could cope with the cold adequately.

Theodore wished she did not take her own strict abstinences and inflict them on the whole household. After all, he reasoned that God had given man fire to keep himself warm. He focussed on the face of his friend Douglas. 'My dear friend, you are awake at last! How are you feeling this morning?' the Reverend asked, as he felt Theodore's forehead with the back of his hand. 'No temperature, good.'

'Wretched, if I am absolutely honest, absolutely wretched! Did you catch Chase? He gave me a good kicking and nearly murdered me,' Theodore said angrily, then looked the other way, slightly ashamed that he felt so bitter. 'He thinks I told the authorities about their last smuggling venture. He had kegs of brandy hidden on a ship, with silk, tea and playing cards. He thought I told on them. As if I would! I tried to tell him that it wasn't me but he wouldn't listen. He just kept on about teaching me a lesson that I wouldn't forget.'

'You mean it wasn't you who told them?' Douglas asked, and Theodore looked at him crest-fallen that his friend should sound so surprised.

'No, although right now I wish I had. They deserved it. To be smashed by the authorities — I mean, by the Revenue men. Did you really think it was me too?'

'Theodore the word in the village was that it was you.' Douglas fidgeted on his chair, obviously ill at ease.

'You mean you knew, and accepted it was me without so much as even asking me to account for myself or deny it?' Theodore asked Douglas as Leticia entered with a maid carrying a tray.

* * *

The tray on which was a warm drink for Theodore was placed on the bedside table. The maid dipped a little curtsey and left. Leticia remained.

Douglas looked at him, 'I'm sorry that I doubted you, but I could not blame you if you had. They are lawbreakers and dangerous men. In a way I suppose I admired the resolve to serve the law no matter what the consequence of the action was.' Douglas looked down at his hands that he was holding on his lap.

'That maybe, but the honest truth of the matter is — I didn't, I never said a word to them,' Theodore answered.

'If it wasn't you, then who did? It had

to be someone who had knowledge of the conversations that have taken place within this house.' Douglas looked at the door as if he was considering the possibility that it might be the maid.

'Yes, it was. I did!' Leticia's voice cut through the air like a knife. She was standing in the middle of the room, by the end of Theodore's bed, her head held high, clasping her small Bible to her.

'It was you, Leticia?' Douglas looked upon her in what Theodore could only describe as shocked disbelief.

'Yes, and I told the press gang about the meeting with those rabble rousers and that irresponsible friend of yours, Montgomery!' Her nose tilted upwards slightly. She looked utterly defiant and proud of her actions regardless of what pain they had caused.

'Whyever would you interfere in other folks business and risk the life of two of my very dear friends, not to mention that of my brother, Brian?' Douglas looked at her bewildered.

'Because those people were smugglers and machine breakers, and your friend was conspiring with them to disobey the law of our country.' Her explanation was simple and sincere, if not misguided, but she was justified in her own eyes.

'Leticia, Montgomery was trying to stop them. He wanted to talk to their leaders before things became uncontrollable. He was trying to save his father's mills and the lives of deprived men. You interfered in what you did not understand, without consulting me, your husband. I am truly shocked.' Douglas looked at her most sternly.

'I was not to know that!' Leticia explained. Her demeanour became a little more insecure than it had been before.

'You have eavesdropped on private conversations, meddled where you should have stayed silent and caused this,' he pointed to the bruises on Theodore's face. 'You should reread that book you hold.'

Leticia gasped as her husband had

never spoken to her so firmly before in their long marriage, but Douglas ignored her and turned back to his friend. 'I can only apologise on her behalf, Theodore. Both you and Montgomery have suffered beatings because of my wife's misplaced sense of 'duty', it is unforgivable.'

'No, Douglas, it is, when the apology is made . . . sincerely.' Theodore looked at Leticia, whose cheeks now burned crimson. Her eyes darted from Douglas to Theodore and back.

'Well, woman?' Douglas asked, 'Are you too proud to apologise for your own mistakes?'

'I . . . I . . . thought,' Leticia began, but Douglas was not having any more discussion on the subject.

'We know what you thought,' he said.

'I am sorry that my actions, no matter how well intended, should have resulted in yourself being hurt in this most brutal way.' Leticia waited for a cursory nod of acceptance from Theodore. Then both men watched her, as she decided to depart, in a fluster without her normal determined stride.

'Women!' Theodore said angrily.

'No,' said Douglas. 'Woman. She is only one, they're not all the same.'

'I'll take your word for it, Douglas. Personally I can never understand their ways — nor do I want to.'

The maid returned for the tray, without her mistress there watching her every move. She approached the bedside table. Theodore quickly drank the lukewarm liquid, grateful for it none the less. She smiled at Theodore and tucked his sheet neatly around him. 'Feeling a little better are you, sir?' she asked.

He smiled at her. 'Yes, Beth, with much thanks to your tender care.'

She giggled. 'You are a tease, sir.' She left the room with the tray, still smiling at him.

'Don't you?' Douglas asked, but Theodore just winked at his friend, yawned and closed his eyes once more.

19

The wagon trundled along the road. The town was just beyond the edge of the moors, down a steep bank into the vale. Maggie had made herself look as respectable as she could, although she felt far from it.

She had not doubted the sincerity of Montgomery's proposal, she had never yet seen him within his own family, or his home surroundings. What if she was far too common for them? She might stand out instantly for what she was — a fallen woman! What if his father hated her on first sight?

Her thoughts seemed to repeatedly go over the same scenes playing out in her head. She imagined a great hall, a crystal chandelier, women gathered for an assembly wearing fine silk gowns.

Then the leader of the household entered the vast hall, broad of girth, proud in stature and a person to reckon with; a self-made man, with new money and seeking a match amongst old moneyed families to gain respectability for his only heir.

Then she realised the figure she visualised in her mind was none other than that of Captain Chase, only he was washed and dressed in fine clothes and had adopted the refined air of an educated man. His unyielding nature was the same, though, in every way.

'We'll soon be there.' Montgomery interrupted her depressing thoughts and removed his protective arm from around her waist. He straightened his own posture, adjusting his coat, fastening all the buttons so that he had to sit erect and proud. She wondered if he had been thinking similar thoughts to her own.

Perhaps the reality of what they had done had sunk in and already he was ready to withdraw his offer. But then he spoke to her, in a tenderly caring voice.

'Don't worry about a thing, Maggie.

If my father disinherits me, I already have land and means of surviving on my own. Our future is secure, but I should like to have his blessing before we decide whether to stay or to leave for our own home.' He patted her leg, and then squeezed it gently in his hand. He released her and held the reins firmly.

'Your own land, Montgomery. Where is that?' Maggie was intrigued as her chosen partner had much more to him than she would have realised.

'Wales,' he answered, simply. But he was smiling mischievously and Maggie sensed there was much more to his statement than appeared from his simple comment.

'Wales?' she repeated.

'Yes, New South Wales, in the colonies.' He laughed as her mouth dropped open. His expression and hers soon changed as they reached the brow of the moor road and headed down into a vale. A cloud, a thick black one could clearly be seen above the town. There was a big fire burning by the river, over a mill in the distance.

'The mill!' he shouted, and tried to convince the old nag to move faster.

'Damnation, I'm too late, it's started already. Now we have returned to a revolution. God help us!'

* * *

The wagon lumbered down into the town. There was chaos as people fled in fear of their lives.

'Where is my father?' Montgomery shouted to a man who had organised a chain of people ferrying buckets of water from the river to the mill.

'Oh, sir, thank God you have returned in time. He is by the mill. He's a broken man, sir. We need you to take charge.' Montgomery forced the frightened animal closer to the mill. Through the smoke-filled air and the people he could see the outline of his father, staring motionless as his precious mill burned.

Montgomery dismounted, leaving Maggie holding the reins. She struggled to steady the tired animal but held it firmly.

'Father! Father!' Montgomery placed his arm around his father's shoulders. 'I'm here, come with me. I'll see what can be done to save it. Come.'

He gently but determinedly steered him away from the burning building and to the wagon.

His father looked at Montgomery. 'You warned me, but I wouldn't listen to him, now all is lost!' His father's shocked expression touched Maggie as Montgomery helped him up next to her.

'Maggie will take you back to the hall,' Montgomery looked at her and said, 'Follow the road, you can't miss it. It is a Jacobean house.'

'Take care, Montgomery, please,' Maggie said, and saw his father's eyes focus on her as she spoke with more familiarity than that of a stranger to his son.

'Go, I must organise this mayhem, then I shall return to you. Make yourself at home and take care of him. He is in a state of shock.'

Maggie steered the wagon away from the town and followed the road until they reached the gates of a large manor house. She stared in amazement at the fine building and then turned to Montgomery's father. 'Is this 'home' sir?'

'Yes, not bad for the son of a baker is it, lass?' He looked at it as if he was studying it anew. 'Do you know, lass, until today, I don't think I've ever viewed it like you are since the day I bought it. You know it's right what the Good Book says. It isn't having money that's a sin, but the love of it.

'God forgive me, I had enough but I fell in love with the notion of having more and more. Those poor folk in the mill, I think some may have been killed.' A tear ran down his face making its way across a soot covered cheek.

'Sir, I think it's time you went home.

Montgomery will do what he can for the people. He has their best interests at heart.' She flicked the reins and took the old wagon along the long drive.

'Yes, he always did have, but I never listened to him. Pride you know.' His voice trailed off as he looked at her studying her face closely. 'Who are you, lass?'

'My name is Maggie Chase, sir. I'm a friend of your son's. But I believe we should leave formal introductions to Montgomery, once the crisis has been sorted out. Don't you?' She looked at his tired back as they pulled up in front of the moated house.

'Perhaps you're right. You have met me at my worst moment, I'm afraid, friend of my son.' Then he jumped down, but before the footman joined them he glanced back and added, 'Or perhaps, at my best.'

They stared at each other for a moment, before the reins were taken from her, and Maggie realised that beyond the dictates of civil society, in those few moments together, she had met the real man, her fiancé's true father. Although he was downhearted and somewhat broken, she liked the person she saw.

20

It was nearly six hours later when Montgomery finally arrived back at the hall. She had been allowed to refresh herself and eat, although her appetite was lacking.

His father had busied himself sending messengers back and forth so they had not spent any further time together as they both anxiously awaited Montgomery's return.

As Montgomery entered the old stone hall, decorated with armour from bygone civil wars, he was greeted from two different directions by the two people who had become the closest and most important people in his whole life.

'Montgomery, are you all right?' the greeting came from Maggie and his father at the same time.

The father looked at his son, who

in turn was looking at Maggie. He embraced her, openly and fondly. Transferring dirt from his coat to her only dress, but neither cared.

He looked at his father, once Maggie was secure in his arms. 'Yes, I'm fine, and thanks to Bill Walmer, no lives were lost.'

'Thank God. Oh Montgomery, we shall rebuild, but it will never be like it was before. It will be better. I shall listen to you, I swear.' He patted Montgomery's back. 'You'll stay, won't you, lad? Don't run off across the world, not yet a while anyhow.'

Montgomery looked at Maggie and raised a smudged eyebrow. 'Should we stay, Maggie?'

She glanced at the worried face of his father, and smiled. 'Yes, I think so, but the new mill will need a school.'

Montgomery laughed, as all three embraced.

The negative images of Montgomery's home that Maggie had built up in her mind disappeared and for once they were replaced with visions of a better future for all — especially hers.

THE END

Other titles in the
Linford Romance Library:

AT SEAGULL BAY

Catriona McCuaig

When Florence Williams and her sister Edie inherit houses at Seagull Bay they decide to set themselves up as seaside landladies, catering to summer visitors. There, Florence's daughters become mixed up with two wildly unsuitable young men. Flattered by the attentions of an unscrupulous entertainer, Vicky tries to elope, but is brought back in time. Having learned that holiday romances seldom last, her prim sister, Alice, wonders if true love will ever come her way.

A TIME TO RUN

Janet Whitehead

When nurse Lynn Crane finds employment at an isolated manor house in the Yorkshire countryside, all is not what it seems. As she nurses her attractive patient, Serge Varda, Prince of Estavia, an alarming truth emerges: her employers, Max Ozerov and the sinister Dr Miros, his countrymen, plan to wrest control of the country from him. The young couple escape from almost certain death, but, as Serge is eventually restored to state duties, will he share them with Lynne?

PRESCRIPTION FOR HAPPINESS

Patricia Posner

From their very first meeting, sparks fly between Rose and Matthew. But they soon discover they have a lot in common — both are coping with loss, and both have a parentless child to love and care for. Their young nieces become best friends, and want nothing more than for all of them to become a family. But even though Rose and Matthew help each other through tough times, neither of them are sure they can get over their past hurts to love again . . .